THE CHINABERRY TREE

BY

JACQUELYN R. THRASH

ROSEBUD PRESS, SAGINAW, MI

THE CHINABERRY TREE

BY

JACQUELYN R. THRASH

The Chinaberry Tree

ACKNOWLEDGMENTS

Scriptural excerpts printed from Thomas Nelson's NKIV Holy Bible by permission for less than fifty quotations. I thank God Almighty who made room for the utilization of all my gifts. Love; grace, peace and more than enough, orchestrate this life given to one of Mississippi sod. May this mainstream novel reach many souls, lift many spirits in the give and take of life.

Special thanks and great gratitude to Brandi D. Thrash and Suzette Perry for the layout, transcription, and the grand design of this fiction novel. Our collaboration honed another great title. The simmering South has come to life on these pages and the Chinaberry's picturesque covers.

Thank you so much models Robert W. Thrash, Daniel and Aaron Phipps, De'Niel and Brandi Phipps. My dear "fav" seven I thank you muchly. What a tremendous blessing and support you are to me.

To my tremendous readership I extend a very special thanks. Photographs by Robert W. and author Jacquelyn Thrash.

The Author

This novel is born of fiction despite the incidence of well-known names.

The Author

ISBN-9:0-9625247-11-x
Copyright
Rosebud Press, Saginaw, MI 48602

The Chinaberry Tree
OTHER BOOKS IN PRINT

The Plight of the African American Male

So Many Names for Jesus

Brody Bates Choice

Born Under the Veil

Secret Hearts

A Piece of Heaven

Heaven's Thunder

A Rose from Ashes

An Ever Changing Life

Shakers, Sharks, & Saviors: Short Stories for the Soul

The Chinaberry Tree

The Chinaberry Tree

Dedicated to Kimberley D., Brandi, and her boys: Daniel O., Aaron Michael, and De'Asia. Always love and revere the Creator.

The Author

The Chinaberry Tree

As iron sharpens iron, so man sharpens the countenance of his friend. Those who keep the fig tree shall eat its fruit; as he who waits on his master will be honored."

Proverbs 27:17-18
Holy Bible

So revelations come!
The Author

The Chinaberry Tree

PREFACE

The life of Haywood Jennings, Jr. was honed and sharpened, even spoke upon years before he'd ventured to the Midwest. This was a great beginning for him, prophesied by his endearing Uncle Joseph Love. Has someone spoken goodness on your mantle? Are you guided by strong beliefs and favor of your Creator?

A great man knows he's cleared every hurdle in life favored by our Maker. The teachings and reachings he's received are spoken in turn to his children's children. It is the legacy of loving parents; as well as positive instruction given by a favored uncle.

Haywood operates in this belief even unto gifting his sons as well. A good father touches the projection of the forehead, and speaks great blessings; from father to son. "Man is sharpening man; iron sharpens iron." (Proverbs 27:17)

The genealogical line of successful productivity is extended in such an act. For Haywood Jennings, Jr., these teachings and extollings take place over seven summers. The Southern connection meets with Haywood's Midwest family over a long period of time.

The revered uncle reveals much under the Chinaberry Tree; shade for some; a nuisance to others; as it's fruit is poisonous to all animals save birds and guinea fowl. In the 1800s numerous vegetative imports are supplanted in the Southeast United States. Their purposes were numerous; to feed cattle, bale livestock, beauty, fruit, and others for medicinal reasons.

The statuesque Chinaberry Tree, "a-mile-a-minute" Kudza, (ge'gen), moss, and bamboo are but a few invasions from Southeast China. The unchecked running rails of growth have created an annoyance to the forestry preserves. All sprout easily; and are hard with which to restrain and contain.

The Chinaberry Tree

The purplish blooms of the Chinaberry are beautiful; then give way to orangey odiferous stink berries only "drunken fowl" eat then lurch about like drunken imbibers. How often they witnessed such spectacles.

Under the Chinaberry Tree Haywood and his doting uncle observe the drunken fowl lurch about. There each simmering summer, Haywood is shaped from the predilections of Joe Love. He is a man of God, two steps from the pulpit; the foibles of life weighing him down. "Pass it on," is his purpose; and Haywood is his chosen heir; his captive audience.

This compelling tale is an extension of short story: "Shakers, Sharks, and Saviors: Ships Worth Knowing." Haywood and Justine are married. They begot three children. He soon fulfills many promises made to her. He has "caught his calling" and is answering God in resounding fervor. Each have gone from Jennings to Jesus. Haywood evolves as a man with a mission. He is walking up the King's Highway!"

The Chinaberry Tree
POST PROLOGUE

"This is my double portion," I concluded as I gaze upon all God has gifted me. "I shall be a great steward over all." I resolve as I proceed to the precipice of a steep hill overlooking the vastness of the valley below.

How much has he answered in my life! Why wouldn't I answer his clarion call? My whole life was laid out leading to this moment in time. It is true; He shall favor all who will follow, obey his principles, and keep Him first in all matters.

Briefly I retreat and turn back enroute to our home where Justine awaits me. I've married a virtuous woman. She is the best of the best! Jus' tends our children; and I am in love with all she does to make our house a home.

No matter how long it took Jus and I are together; one in the eyes of God. When He sees me, He sees her. Most of my life I've dreamed of this day. We've gone through much. Seven years of marriage have given us three beautiful replicas of us. Haywood III and Harrison are the spitting image of me and our daughter is the exact image of Justine.

"Wow!" I think then exclaim aloud, "Two green eyed, tawny haired girls!" I step up my pace. My morning constitution is almost done. Breakfast awaits me.

Jus' waves to me from the patio. Aurelia peers through the sieves of the screened porch mimicking her mother. Strong aromatic smells of just made breakfast prompts me to pick up the pace.

"Breakfast's ready," Jus' says as I hold her closely to me.

"That's good to know, Little Woman," I reply and begin to remove my aged brown parka and earth-clotted shoes. She re-enters our home pulling Auri after her. I pause briefly pondering whether I should drop any more plans on her.

"Pastor's asked me to bring the message every third Sunday."

"Oh, really? You've only been studying for a time."

The Chinaberry Tree

"Dr. Sloan thinks I'm more than ready. I think so too! I eat, sleep, and mentally ingest theoneutics. It's second nature now, Jus'."

"Okay! I called you Minister before you'd begun. We are truly blessed. God on our side is a given."

"I thought you'd think I'd give up our times together."

She pecked me on the cheek. "No, you're pretty religious about all you undertake."

I am drawn into minister; yet just as strongly I'm drawn to my Southern beginnings. Uncle Joe taught me much; even foretold of my being a man of God, fully committed.

"I have much to ponder," I conclude as I joined them at the table. Our sons fidget; Aurelia claps her hands as Jus' hands her a biscuit. Blessed food prompts the boys to pile their plates high, ready to dig in. Soon we all dig in with a spattering of light wit. Among giggles, grins, and chewing I ask myself once more: "Why you want to uproot them from their familiar?"

"Hay! Earth to Hay! What you thinking about Hay? I called you three times!"

"We're going south soon," I blurted out.

"A visit to your franchises?" She asked

"How about a trip to see Aunt Carrie, Ferndale and all of them?" I finished excitedly.

"Mississippi. How soon?" Not really for it, four puzzled faces return my gaze. Jus' seemed staunchly opposed just as she'd been when I'd decided to plant two Chinaberry trees near the terrace. I reassured them, set them at ease.

Come on guys! It'll be fun. I'll get a van. It'll be scenic; a real vacation. Did I ever take you anywhere that wasn't alright?"

"Okay, Hay! When? How long?"

The Chinaberry Tree

"Soon, Jus'! Real soon."

The idea to venture south received a lukewarm reception. The south was slowly snapping back from strong hurricanes and violent tornadoes.

"Everything's everything!" I say clasping Jus' small left hand in mine.

It's just the way it is. It's been a while coming; but the plan is they'd agree. I will always protect my little family. Much is drawing me there. Overtime I described Uncle Joe's farm as paradise. Then realized seeing is believing. My mind takes me there often, to terraced lands, fecundous growth of China's imports, project a picturesque beauty hard to describe. Later I approach Jus' at the sink, intent on putting away just-washed breakfast dishes I hug her close and reiterate: "It'll be fine, My Little Woman!"

The Chinaberry Tree

BOOK I

FLASHBACK TO LOVE

AUGUST 2002

The Chinaberry Tree

Hay and I are one; and I, Justine Aurelia Jones am singing a new song of contentment. For a time I sat in a huge brown velvet chair. I felt I belonged there in Hay's huge cavernous bedroom; a place just right for his tall statuesque frame. I watched him hug his pillow as if he were still holding me. He is at peace; and so am I. My mind is flooded by events of the past eight hours.

"There's nothing to fear, Jus' I will never harm you," he'd repeated.

Hay turned over and searched the bed for me. "Jus' where'd you go?"

"I'm here," I answered inaudibly.

"What you doing way over there? Come back to bed." I didn't obey him; which is a rarity for me. I shook my head "no." He scrambled across then came to me, lifted me effortlessly. He set me down in the stall and turned on deluxe spray from many directions.

"Finally, Jus, we can shower together."

"What I wanted to do at the Hilton Gardens," I'd agreed.

"I know that!" He answered. We moved into spray from all directions. It was natural to move closer to him; my wet hair plastered over my shoulders, I was fully aware of the charged effect the whole experience had on us. He soon handed me a bath sheet that draped to my ankles, then donned another that came to his calves. He held me tightly.

"This is better than the Hilton. There's none but you and I and this moment in time."

"I knew it would be like this!"

"Okay, Mr. Worldly Man!"

"No! No! Jus, this is a once in a lifetime thing, Sweet Thang!"

"Sweet Thang!?"

"The absolute sweetest, Mon Amie!"

"Oh, no, Frenchy! Speaka-the-English!"

The Chinaberry Tree

"Oh contraire, Madame Jennings to be!"

"Can't wait! You're a man who keeps promises." I chuckled at the irony of it.

"Are you okay?"

"I'm quite fine," I answered, my heart beat wildly at the thought of us together.

"Make plans, Jus'! I want you with me always."

"It's a deal!" As time passed we talked endlessly. I felt closer than I'd ever been with anyone else. Around ten am I rose to leave. He pulled me back down. "What's your Saturday routine?"

"Oh' I'll think of you, replace vituals, shoot a few hoops; think of you; run a few errands; and oh, yes, did I say, think of you?"

"Ha! Ha! When you hook up with Mel and all those super jocks all you'll think of is lay ups and baskets!"

"Well now! I'm still trying to keep up with you! What else is on that fine mind of yours?"

I looked him squarely in the eyes. "Take me to see the new James Bond film at the Capital. Love me some James Bond!"

Hay returned my gaze then feigned jealousy. "Just how should I feel about my woman getting all gushy over my competition?"

"Pierce is fierce!" I answered tearing myself away from him. He rose to follow and I seized the opportunity to tear the bedding off the huge bed.

"Where's your hamper?" I asked dragging the king sized sheets towards the enclosure in which he pointed.

"Whew!" I said feeling winded.

"This is a fresh start on your day!"

"Like I needed that!" He said a smile on his face.

The Chinaberry Tree

"Jus', you look every bit of seventeen. How old are you now?"

"You know very well I'm twenty-nine!"

"Wow! You're getting' on, girl!"

"I'm getting' dressed," I said quickly donning all the emerald dressing I'd worn to the county fair.

"Stay, lady, stay!" He said following me.

"Oh no you don't! I've got chores before you pick me up at seven, Mr. Spoiled Man!"

"It's a date! Won't be late!" He sang. I turned and tackled him, now fully dressed.

"You are so spoiled, Haywood!"

He shook his head "no." "Nooo! No, I'm not!"

"For real. Whatever you want; whatever you need I'll supply it naturally…"

We were overcome with giggles. His embrace was just a bit too tight.

"I'm not letting you go, Jus'! I got you now!"

"You just take these tentacles off me! Gotta run, My Man!" He chased me around the bed and caught me. We fell back on the mattress still laughing wildly. I know now he not only wanted me to open up to him; he's thoroughly enjoying the pull and tug of play.

"We always seem to end up here, but you've got to take me home, Monsour Super Jock!"

"What will you do while I'm away?" he asked.

"Oh, I'll think of you; clean my abode; shop 'til I drop; think of you; listen to our favorites; write a little; then of course, think of you!"

"Sounds like a winner to me!"

"I couldn't stop if I wanted to; I mean winning with you!"

The Chinaberry Tree

Hay rose slowly. It seemed to take forever for him to dress in sweats, even tie his huge tennis shoes.

"You know, Hay!" I said ignoring his slow methodical movements trying to slow up the inevitable.

"We're going deep now! I can see it coming!"

"I was just thinking how colors, numbers, thoughts and ideas are floating around above us, just ready for someone to reach up and retrieve them; put them to use."

"Uh, Huh! And that means?"

"I've read statements I've thought or written used by other writers. I had no connection to them; was never in their presence when they'd conjured these ideas."

"All has been rehashed, rephrased and reused. I think the adage is 'there's nothing new under the sun.' I've been in meetings, even in church, and ideas come to me and I don't act on them. Then someone else proposes that self same idea. Right now you want to take my mind off what you feel I'm thinking. Right?"

"No, I don't Hay!"

"You sure protest too vigorously, 'Maid Marian', green-eyed scholar in Robin Hood Emerald."

"I'm not thinking that at all!"

Once more we sat very closely together. "I've got you now, and I'm not letting you go! It's our time. I'm glad I waited…didn't hook up with anyone else. It's you I've always wanted. Sometimes I'm so bowled over by you I put distance between us; get busy, tied up, even. It's like coming up for air. Girl, you make me nervous!"

"You were like a stand-up comedian; making me laugh to lighten many moods!" We gazed into each other's souls.

The Chinaberry Tree

"Stay here with me, Justine!"

"I know you, Hay! It's all mutual. We'll see each other later, Okay?"

"I don't have to see you later; I have you now!" He's so strong. I struggled to be free.

"You want me to stay, but we've got..."

"Don't say 'all the time...'"

"I wasn't!"

"Then what?"

"To me last night was our wedding night. We'll be married; dance to our favorites; live a great life together. It's all a given."

"My sweet lady, nothing is ever lost that cannot be regained. Our time is not God's time. He sits outside this moveable creation. He knows just when a matter should evolve and unfold unto fruition. You're greater to me than any trophy I've ever won." So insistent he tried to undress me. I sprang up, grabbing bear and my purse, then moved quickly to the living room.

He followed. "Wait up!"

"You are so spoiled, Haywood!"

"Look whose talking!" He answered grabbing his keys.

"I am not at all!"

"I know, Hay. That is profoundly true. Just joshing! God had you waiting for me, but in another place, Brother Minister!"

"Together, Justine, we'll move mountains. Just you wait!"

"Awright, then, I'll see you at seven," I ended opening the door.

He hugged me again. It was difficult to remove myself. Rudyard Kipling's poem "If" came to mind.

"If you can keep your head..." I began. Hay finished the line.

"When all around you others are losing theirs..."

The Chinaberry Tree

"If!"

"Yes, 'If'! That's my favorite poem. I used to recite it to myself often. It's how I kept my head about me; that poem and my Bible helped me not get caught up in all that hype! I became a man, just as Uncle Joe predicted I would. I put away childish things; connected with my inner man; shunned the 'holic' life.

"Holics...?!"

"You know wild women, drugs, drink, gamin' and playin' the field! The flow of mounds of money created many possibilities. You have much, way above the fray; at the top of your game, nothin' can touch you! I saw it jade many for life. The way back to one's self was next to impossible."

"How did you surpass the excess with such a strong draw on you?"

"My faith saved me from many perils. I had a belief system. They called me 'Deacon' cause I always carried 'the Word' and prayed before every game. As I turned to God, I had to be strong."

"I'm glad you did, Hay! You came to me correctly. You are just whom I'd needed in my life."

"Mel told me so much about you. I knew I had to come for you. He said you were kind of reclusive."

"I was writing. It's a solitary venture. Anyhow Mel didn't know everything!" He raised a brow. I started to giggle.

"What? What's so funny?"

"This long, long, long kiss good day!"

"Very funny, Jus'! Why I oughta...!"

"Never let me go!" I ended, hugging him firmly; not wanting him to leave my door.

"See you soon," he said.

The Chinaberry Tree

"It's a given," I answered closing the door; stepping into my familiar surroundings. Bear was stashed on my favorite cushy accent chair. Within minutes I'd curled up on the couch with a cup of green tea, my PJs replaced all that green. Mulling over the events of the previous encounter I felt too agitated, to ecstatic to fall asleep. It's so marvelous! I'm one with one of the most glorious suitors I've ever encountered.

"Mrs. Haywood Jennings Jr." I said aloud. "It's going to happen!" I became the 'picture poster' for huge grins. "Oh Mistress Fate, don't shake me, wake me! The impossible has happened in just seven months."

The decision to venture to bed came next. I could not get past all this giddiness.

"Mrs. Haywood Jennings Jr.," I repeated.

Soon I was drifting under fresh crisp linen, slipping into much needed rest; though my thoughts were continually crowded with his image; and my body ached as though I'd wrestled a thousand bears; it all was par for the course. My wedding night was last night. I am one with the man sent to me by God. I'd prayed for something real; Hay truly fits the bill!

"Goodnight, Hay," I say and drift into slumber.

****

Wrens and morning doves have set up good "nest-keeping" outside my window. Their incessant chirping awakened me hours later. The radio clock read twelve noonish. Still I remained lolled under warm covers. Impulsively I lifted the nearby receiver and quickly dialed. He answered right away.

"I'm glad you rang me!"

"Hey! Hey, Hay! Are you awake also?"

"I was just about to call you; but you beat me to the 'purnch'," he said slurring the word "punch" ebonically.

The Chinaberry Tree

"Oh, no! Don't start, Hay!"

"What?"

"You want to keep me giggling like a silly teen!"

"I thought you liked it when I made you laugh!"

"I do. Be serious! When do I see you again?"

"Can't I come over now? Do you miss me as well?"

"Yes, I do, but we have so much to do! Should we chuck our normal Saturday activities?"

"What? What will you do till we meet again?"

"Play some jazz, some Sade, clean my condo; think of you; replace staples; run some errands…Oh yes! Think of you!"

"Beautiful xanthic woman of mine I expect you to do no less. I'm inspired by just knowing you belong to me! What can I bring you when I come later?"

"Just you, you, and you!":

"Come over here right now!" Hay commanded.

"Oh no! Gotta run! See you soon great Lothario that I love!"

"You've got so much power over me, Jus'!"

"You are spoiled, bon homme!"

"It's a given to whom much is given, much is required."

"I don't think *that* is what that scripture means."

"Come back to me, Jus'! He said softly.

"Raincheck!" I answered and quickly hung up.

****

"Does everyone know I'm in love?" I thought inwardly when cashier Ben compliments me.

"Is someone having a party, Miss Jones?"

"No party, my friend!"

The Chinaberry Tree

"I meant the wine, Miss Jones!"

"Well 'invitas veritos'; In wine there is truth!" He bagged the chilled Magnum of Asti, then insisted on delivering my sacks to my car. I tried to tip him. He refused the tip.

"See you soon! He's a mighty lucky man!"

"Are you flirting, Ben?" He grew pink from neck to cheek.

"No, ma'am! Just voicing an observation!"

The wine acquisition was a mere whim; my intent to toast our engagement. Minutes later I returned home, put away my groceries, and then tackled my slightly disheveled surroundings. By three I'm done. The phone toned soon after.

"Jus', are you done? I'm done. Can I come over now?"

"You thinking of catching an earlier matinee?"

"No; but it's very important."

"Sure. Okay. I'm done!"

Twenty minutes later he was at my door, all dapper in the navy shirt and slacks I'd bought him in Columbus' Easton Open Air Mall. I hugged him. "I knew you'd look great in this ensemble. The cardigan finishes it off."

"Okay! Okay!" he feigned discomfort.

"I know you'll look great in blue also!"

"I don't have time to change. Just been relaxin' and waxin'!"

"Can we be serious for a minute?"

"Okay!" I wiped the smile from my lips in a swipe.

He placed a jewel box in my hands. I opened the box to a sparkling diamond blue topaz ring. He slid it on my right ring finger.

"May I wear it on the left?"

"Either. Whatever you like! We'll pick your engagement ring soon."

"You did say everyday is Christmas. I believe it now."

The Chinaberry Tree

"Glad you're pleased. No protest?"

"Not-a-one! It's very wonderful! I'll get dressed. Help yourself to stuff in the fridge."

"No, I'm fine, thanks," he replied and settled himself on the sofa, channel-surfing sports.

"Be back soon," I said entering my bedroom, and then racing to my closet. I picked Baby Blue topped with Heaven's Blue slacks and shirt, topped by a Baby Blue Pea Jacket. Blue suede wedges made me taller. I soon returned with my wallet and keys, thrusting my ring finger in my pocket to stop ogling the dazzling ring.

"We sure match, Justine!"

"In more ways than one, Bon homme! Hay, please pray for us that we stay this happy forever. It's scary!" He took my hand and led me to my front door.

"Our Lord will favor whomever I favor. It's a given, Jus'!"

****

"Hello, James! Here we come!" I effused as we prepared to enter traffic that seemed exceptionally busy. Henry Wadsworth Longfellow said it best: "We are not ships that pass in the night, never speaking afterwards." We have stopped our moors closely docked, exploring and soaring towards a life together. Life is so grand!

"Together Forever" played softly on Sirrius Jazz. Much more than a coincidence, Hay and I are together forever. Great times seem imminent. No more fears; no more tears; I have gone from "J" to "J"; from Jones to Jennings.

"Mr. Gorgeous Man, are you as excited about James as I?"

"How and why should I get excited about my competition?"

"It's just a picture, Hay!" He feigned disinterest.

****

The Chinaberry Tree

An SRO crowd gathered. The lobby burgeoned with movie goers; flowing into three showing rooms. Broccoli's cinematic action drama didn't disappoint the onlookers. The chief villainy was a daunting duo bent on amassing hordes of conflict diamonds to build a massive sun-charged destructive laser contraption, hung from the firmament in billowing displays. Explosions cast diamond constellations in villainous, tall Zaul's right complexion. "James, Oh James" went to a Korean Prison, tortured, stung, revived; all to go through such ordeals numerous times in his fourteen month stay.

"Pierce is so fierce!" I'd effused once more as he seeks Zaul and Gustav to execute his revenge. I clutched at, pummeled, and drew Hay into all that non-stop action. I was not disappointed. I am a James Bond fan!

"What can we say about that Halle? I mean Jynx?" Hay whispered, undoubtedly making me a bit jealous as well. Later we discussed it while negotiating a larger than exiting crowd.

"Broccoli's 'rock 'em; sock 'em' non stop energy did not disappoint me."

"That scene with Halle walking out of the Atlantic surf is a repeat of Ursula Andress' scene in 'Thunderball'," Hay compared.

"Were you just watching Halle?"

"No. Just making note that some of the scenes were updated to fit the time. Some have been used before."

"Know thy enemy?"

"No, Jus'! He is just a character; albeit extremely popular." He looked around us. "There will be more! Promise you'll take me," I'd asked as we neared the exit.

"It's a done deal. One day very soon I'll even take you to Spain, Paris, St. Tropez, Asia. Yeah! Ah, yeah! Iceland. Perhaps stay in one of those iceberg hotels."

The Chinaberry Tree

"Well, Mr. Gorgeous Man, I'll believe it when I see it! Anyway I'd never get warm even in a mound of fur. I could feel the cold!"

"There are many ways to keep warm," Hay answered raising his brow suggestively.

"I shall repeat: You are so spoiled!"

"Jus' where is your mind?"

"Haywood!" Tall statuesque Beverly exclaimed.

"Hi, Bev! Mel with you?"

"Yes. He's fetching the SUV."

"Justine, you remember my charming sister-in-law, Beverly?"

"Hi, Jus'! I've told Hay to bring you around!" I was once again surrounded by two tall "trees", hugged in the midst of them. Released, Bev continued her rap.

"I've told Hay to bring you by, Justine!"

"Real soon," Hay answered now smiling broadly down at both of us.

"Why you jokin', Hay?" I whispered.

"Who me?" He asked ushering us close to the exit. Bev entered their dark van. The brothers nodded.

"My place or yours?" He asked as we returned farewell waves.

"Mine, please." I'd suggested. Twenty minutes later we were there. Hay grabbed the remote and settled on the sofa. I thought he'd choose sports, but he stopped on BET Jazz. Will Downing serenaded damsels on a white sandy dune.

"Together Forever," has become popular of late.

Minutes later I sat a tray of sandwiches, table grapes, napkins, two goblets, and the chilled bottle of Asti Spumante.

"Wasn't that too heavy?"

"No! I'm tough enough!"

"I know you're right!" He said, taking the bottle, expertly opening it and pouring two goblets halfway.

"Let's toast our future, Hay!"

We clinked glasses as he said, "To us, now, forever, and always!"

"Here! Here!" I said and drank the icy elixir. He poured more wine. I offered food. He shook his head. "Come. Be next to me." I nestled in his arms.
He posed another toast. "To our eternal love and many tomorrows." He said and we drank once more.

"Oooh! It goes right through my veins," I said sinking into soft throw pillows.

"You go right to my head." He set the goblets on the table amongst the food we had not touched.

"Come to me, Justine."

"You know, Hay," I began moving away from the inevitable.

"Let's not make small talk. Just be with me, Jus'." I obeyed. Inhabitions all gone; our incredible, inevitable act of belonging is now happening again. My pulse raced from the nearness and the wine.

"He's my husband," I inwardly thought, but I said, "Oh, Hay, please wait!"

"There's no more waiting. Aren't we past the passionate kiss?"
I nodded, "Yes." He spoke to me softly tenderly. "You are my beloved. Share my life, Justine. I've waited so long for you."

He led the way; and I followed without protest or reservations. On my queen sized bed I said, "Let's pretend."

"There's no more pretending. We are here in this moment of time. You and me. We are one, my love."

He did not leave me that night. The next morn we set a date to order my engagement ring. "You're putting a rush on me!"

"I want us together as man and wife!"

The Chinaberry Tree

****

Our wedding plans now finalized for August thirty-first of two thousand two. My third finger left hand now sports a four carat flawless diamond ring. We are almost never apart. I now thoroughly feel "the endless Christmas" he has proclaimed often enough. Four of my friends are soon vying to become my "maid-of-honor." It's hard to choose. All are very dear to me; even Carla my sister, not to mention Beverly.

"Perhaps I can have two Matrons," I pose later as I speak to Hay.

"Sounds complicated to me, Jus', make a choice!"

I finally picked Dorothy. Once again I complained to Haywood. "I'm trying to keep it simple; but it keeps on expanding," I complained once more to Hay.

"There's no problem, hon! You can have whatever you want. Anyhoo! I opened you an expense account. Is fifty thousand enough?"

"Won't we need that for our home?"

"No. Is that enough?"

"Yes. More than enough, My Endless Santa! Thanks. I really mean thank you muchly!"

"Wow, Jus'! You don't protest anymore!"

"May's well go with the flow, I always say!"

"Uh huh!"

"Anyway our colors are Heaven's Blue, brown and white. Perhaps milk chocolate or cinnamon for you; and blue and white for me. Your tuxes are baby blue with brown lapels and trim, and satin brown cumber buns."

"Whoa, Jus'! You've been busy!"

The Chinaberry Tree

"Time is fast approaching. I made some decisions like you said. I've ordered twelve tall topiaries loaded with white and blue blossoms tied of fine brown
satin ribbons and bows."

"It's all coming together. This is your first big bash you've always wanted to plan for me. I love it already. Be by in a few with that bank book."

"One more thing, Hay! Really two more requests. What do you think of a roped off section of the south lawn of Sullivan?"

"Consider it done! And the second is…?"

"We need three baby blue stretch Lincoln Limos." I kept testing the water. He had not said "no" to anything I'd requested.

"Consider it done, Sweet Thang!"

"I'll be that for you!"

"I know that you will," he ended as we soon ended the call.

****

Finally it was all underway. Unfolding nicely. My maids became indispensable; took care of a thousand space details. At times they'd disappear on me on personal errands.

"Patience be my friend," I concluded as they'd soon come forth finishing much. Briefly I'd think of mother, father, sister and brother. I've been told that those gone on their rewards in Heaven watch over us. I spoke aloud to my mother:

"Dear Mom,

Fate had me lined up as a sheep for slaughter. Hay, helped me, my Sweet Mother! I miss you so very much. I wish you were here. I'm marrying a beautiful and spiritual man like Daddy. He's strong and 'take-charge'. He's my soul mate. God gave me another soul mate. He's rich in goodness. I also suspect he's very well-off. I went through a sad time when I lost you all, but I'm so happy now,

The Chinaberry Tree

Mom! I'm so happy! All the misery has faded. Now I have someone to watch over me in my life. I obey him, Mom! Who'da thunk it? Without reservation, he loves me; and I obey him. I am filled with joy! Love ya'll dearly!

****

"Justine? Where are you girl?" Dot calls me from the doorway, bringing me back to the present.

"I'm right here waiting! Where did all ya'll get off to this time?"

"Just runnin' errands. What's next, bride to be?"

"Our date had to change. We're accommodating many guests. Hay's super jocks are coming."

The decorators soon took over, roped off a special area on the south lawn near the bleachers now freshly painted alabaster. Yards of tarp and artificial grass were soon in place. A tent was suggested numerous times; I adamantly said "no".

We are blessed of God! All worked together for good, September 19th's glorious day. Our Indian Summer's Day evolved clear and bright. Our temps fluxuated between a pleasant sixty-eight to seventy-four degrees. Paradise.

Fifty minutes after the ceremony began I was saying "I do" to Hay. Some say they don't feel any differently, but I was greatly moved as Hay picked me up and "saluted" me as Mrs. Haywood Jennings, Jr.

Contemporary Jazz and wedding mood music was piped on long play til Beverly and Melvin sang a rendition of our theme song, "The First Time I Ever Saw Your face". Three hundred guests including Solomon and Georgia Tisdale, and over half of Hay's pro-ball team and guests favored us also.

Without a Hitch? What hitch? Our party took care of every detail. The ride about, in three soft blue stretch limos were clanking, honking, and reveling for an hour. As we neared the bustling banquet of Monsour's hundreds poured into three entrances. Hay rolled down the window.

The Chinaberry Tree

"Looks like we made it, Madame Jennings!"

"We sure have, Monsour Bon Homme!"

"It's only the beginning. Welcome to my world, Justine!"

Though tears of joy streamed my make-up, we seemed to always be smiling and greeting, then posing for a thousand pictures. We were seated after our dance to "Just One Look!" Hay gave me his hanky from his lapel pocket. "I'm overwhelmed!"

"As I am in you," He said pulling my chair nearer to him. Resounding applause erupted.

"Look! Densburg and staff made it. We rose to greet them as they approached. Gregory handed me an embossed envelope. I hugged each one tightly.

"Open it later when you're alone," Gregory said bussing me on my teary cheeks.

"Is this fodder for another novel, Justine?"

"We shall see, Gregory! Love you. Thanks for always being there."

"Had nothin' better to do." He said lightly.

"Stop! You're joking, Greg!"

"That's rare," Suzette cut in. "He 'never' jokes! It's refreshing!" We all laughed. The wedding party was dwindling; receding slowly. Next we held court for the dwindling crowd, then ran for the dance floor.

****

"Never a moment to ourselves til tomorrow," Hay concluded.

"It doesn't matter! I'm having a blast!" Taking Mel's hand to dance as he drew me out on the floor.

"Well, Mrs. Jennings, how goes it? Better than the County Fair, would you say?"

"Mel, I say that and more! Did I ever thank you for reporting to Hay?"

The Chinaberry Tree

"Who me? I need no thanks. I didn't let him bring home a basketball groupie. He's loved you all our lives. It was in the stars. I had little to do with it. My out-going, won't quit brother made it happen."

"Well I say graciously enough: Thank you Bro-in-Law!"

"You're very welcome! Welcome to the 'tree colony'!"

"Tree Colony?"

"You've married into 'the tall bunch'!" He chuckled.

"You are so zany, Mel!"

"Don't you know it?!"

****

"Ooh! My feet ache so awfully, Hay!" I complained as we took a breather from the floor. Hay tugged my chair closer, took off my stilettos; then produced a gold-embossed box from under his. "For My Wife, a gift of gifts!"

I accepted it, and then tore the gold wrappings away including the satin brown and blue ribbons.

"A promise is kept! Let's hit the road!" The card read.

Round-trip tickets to Paris, London, and St. Tropez were individually tied.

"I'm going to take you to all those places James goes one day!" I recalled his declaration. The time is ours now.

I blubbered some more, alternating between clinging to him and streaming my make-up. My tears were flowing like Niagara Falls.

"How did you get all of this done?"

"Carla and your gal pals were real helpful. It's not easy keeping secrets from you."

"They'd worked through details I'd given them, then disappear on me."

"We shopped for and packed an extensive new wardrobe, all size eight and extra small."

"No matter how, we got it done! I have a trousseau also."

"Bring that along as well. I'm sure you'll need it all. We begin tomorrow!"

"What about rest?"

"We'll get some, but we can always rest on the plane. Come on! Come dance with me, Mrs. Jennings, Jr.!"

A limo delivered us to his condo hours later. He barely got me over the threshold. Suitcases, clothing and such were strewn about all over his/our place.

"How long are we staying?"

"A few days in each country."

"A real James Bond Adventure!"

"I'm not a spy!" Hay defended.

"You sure worked your plan to get us here; right here in this moment. I'd say you know how to make things happen!"

"Looks like we made it, Madame!"

"Looks like there's no space for us."

"Oh, come on! We'll move this, pick up that; put these over there."

He was talking as he moved bundles and cases about.

"Okay!"

"There's so much more you don't know about me Jus'! I'm your new man of mystery. You scared of me, Jus'?"

"No. Not in the least. I know you, Hay!"

"There's more. Non force' le main!"

"What hand am I forcing?"

"Don't worry. It's all good! Look over here!" He held up two oversized blue silk night shirts. We soon donned the two night shirts that made me think of "Scrooge Wear".

"Com'mere, Mrs. Jennings," He ordered.

The Chinaberry Tree

"It's yo body, sugar," he tried to serenade me with those Levert, Brown, and Johnny Gill lyrics.

"You ought to quit!" I answered.

I fell into his arms overcome in giggles. "You gonna join that group?"

"TMI, babe! You're messin' up the romantic mood I'm perpetrating!"

"We don't need no mood!" I said tackling him.

"You're pretty strong for a little woman. That's it, you're my little woman!"

"Incredible. You can call me anything you like."

"What did you call this?"

"Our incredible inevitable."

"Ah, yeah!" Hay answered in total agreement.

****

Fifteen hours later he lifted me over the threshold of our VIP suite near the Champ Elysee. Paris is wonderful. He'd promised Paris. In the next four days we explored Latonas, the garden fountain; our room; then onto Versailles; our room; dined at the top of the Eiffel Tower; oh yes, and our room! Finally we visited the picturesque village of Alsace; and finally rested in our suite before our morning flight to London.

Four days later we lodged near Soho for the extreme London experience. We bought even more from Harrod's, art galleries, clubs, pubs for fish-n-chips.

"What an adventure London is! Yeah! Yeah! Yeah!"

****

Scenic isle; enormous beaches; grand hotels and arenas filled our next four day's visit to St. Tropez. Each Southern France shoreline accommodated all seeking romantic ambiance and roiling surf.

The Chinaberry Tree

Haywood took charge as we checked in our La Plaza suite. Opulence, wealth, and elan created a magical mood. We were surrounded by the bored and super rich. Finally it was our turn. Hay presented a number of credit cards.

"You honor any of these?" Hay inquired.

"Fine, Sir! Each is fine! The suite is two thousand five hundred a night. Any special instructions, Mr. Jennings?"

Before Hay could answer I tugged at his sleeve, pulling him down to whisper. He kissed me instead.

"No! No! No! I don't want a kiss! I mean…not right now!"

"What, Jus'?!"

"Do you need some help? You've spent so much. I have money. Let me help!"

"You are so sweet! I got this, girl!"

"Okay!"

Our luggage filled two carrier carts. In minutes he'd carried me over the fourth threshold. He sat me on a huge plush accent chair. I know to stick and stay when he said, "Be still, Jus'! I have much to show you."

The expensive case lay unlocked on an ottoman. He'd spread numerous print outs, blueprints and legal papers.

"Come see, Jus'!" I came closer. He embraced me. "Jus', we can live very well for a lifetime. I'm worth millions. You know me. I did not squander what I earned. I put my money to work for me. I've invested well; plus these are my two franchises; all doing quite well."

"You own all of this?"

The Chinaberry Tree

"I just sold my mansion for two mil-three. It was spanking brand new. I spent very little time there. We'll live in my condo till our place is finished. I hope you like what I've done. See if you want to make any changes."

"You've put a lot of work into it."

"What do you think?"

"Well, I can live with this!" I pointed to the recreation room.

"I can live with that!" I pointed to the kitchen and adjoining room.

"I can really live with this!" I let my finger linger at the huge master bedroom.

"You ought to quit!" Hay said.

"Jus', you're wearin' me out!"

"Not too much! Like makin' up for lost time."

"Fruit multiply!" I thought sheltered there in his arms.

****

"We'd better hurry up and get babies. I may grow not to share you with anyone!"

"What kind of babies?" Hay asked his interest peaked.

"Little super-jocks tossin' b-balls and getting' into much!"

"How about little golden girls with tawny hair; oh, either would be just fine!"

"I can see it now, hon'! We'll fill Haywood Jennings Lane with those little ones and lots of love and nurturance. We'll grow them up with great care and resolve."

"I'm glad you want to give me children. It's what I love above Mel's and Solomon's life. We could start now!" He raised his brow.

The Chinaberry Tree

We were packing. "Stop, Hay, we've got to get all this stuff to the airport."

"The limo picks us up in an hour," he said.

"Don't give me that look! You are so spoiled, Haywood!"

"Tell me you're not!"

"I'm not," I answer but give into him soon after.

****

"Nine-Eleven." Many travel matters changed with "Nine-Eleven." Our return to American soil was harried, delayed and unsettling. At every juncture we'd been questioned, queried and scrutinized with our multiple luggage. Hay kept our passports visible. He sheltered me. Took the lead; got us through much. Officials with guns and luggage-sniffing-dogs created angst in me. We came to some sober conclusions.

"We'll travel more simply with less baggage in the future," Hay concluded.

Finally, after three hours we were on our way to our next connection. Hay rented a Lincoln Navigator filled with tons of luggage. Home…home coming. I couldn't wait to get home. We soon exited Detroit Metro. In forty-five minutes the sign Beacon County re-energized both of us. We were beyond weary.

"Tell me what was good for you, Justine?"

"We christened every place we stayed as our 'love nest', then again Paris and St. Tropez were wonderful!"

"Oh, my! Ah, yeah! I've created a 'love monster'," Hay joked.

"Hay, you think you so 'bout it; bout it!"

"From whence did that come?"

"Lisa says: 'You're so 'bout it; 'bout it!"

The Chinaberry Tree

"Lisa barely says anything to me!"

"She can be kinda introverted sometimes."

"Not at all like you, My Little Magpie!"

"I got your 'Magpie'! Hay, your mouth runs like the Indy Five Hundred!"

"You talkin' to me, Jus'!"

"Yep!"

"Say somethin' else!" He threatened.

"You're the love of my life!"

"You, too, girl! You've taken over my world."

"And you mine."

"Almost home," Hay announced.

"And not too soon!" I answered, finally understanding why he'd called me "Magpie" I answer him every time.

****

Time has evolved; and I've become firmly ensconced in my roll as wife to a man with many "irons in the fire". How do I handle all of this loot? I rarely speak of it. I am amazed at all he's amassed, even allowed him to invest my residuals. Which are growing quite nicely.

Our lives are full of simple pleasures, similar to those present in our courtship. I wasn't aware then of all he's accumulated, and I'm satisfied with what he shares. He's orchestrated a great life for us. We are endeared to Mel and Beverly, Solomon and Georgia, Mark and Sherita, our Sullivan pals; and Dr. Pastor Sloan and our grand family of faith.

From time to time Hay mentions his southern connection on Joseph Love's Farm. He gets a faraway look when he mentions his Uncle Joe, Aunt Carrie,

The Chinaberry Tree

Cousin Ferndale and his children. Then he offers just one more trip we're going to take.

"You say we're going soon; then you put it off!" He hedges.

"Just haven't taken the time, but we're going, hon."

"Sometimes you speak more about Uncle Joe than anyone else."

"It's Uncle Joe who spoke on my life; instilled in me a great faith. He is so much a part of my beginning. I wish he could have met you; and you him!"

"Does Mel feel as you do?"

"Can't say. Don't know."

"Well, whenever you're ready; we'll go." I answer.

****

Promises are always kept by Haywood, no matter the space of time. Four months after our honeymoon we've moved into our beautiful enormous home. It is more filled with love, closeness, and cooperation. Carla now resides in my condo, and Travis Mead, one of Hay's assistant coaches bought Hay's condo. Hay is the greatest juggler I know. He manages, arranges, oversees, operates, runs, and tends his franchises. We've made two trips to rally the workers. How he does it boggles my mind! All bases are fully covered.

Children…Hay speaks often of children. When I broached the subject he asks pointedly: "You getting' tired of me, Sweet Thang?"

"Tell me again what you'd like," I say as if I can fulfill his request.

"Perhaps tall minor replicas of you with floaty manes, Lil' Hay Jenning's Super Jocks!"

"Now that you put it that way; boys are good! Ah, yeah! Little players of 'the game'!"

The Chinaberry Tree

"We can do more than dream. Let's go back to Paris," I suggest.

"We loved Paris. Now, okay, Paree with a purpose!"

****

Mighty Miracles flow in our lives continually. At some point on that trip we begat our first son, Haywood Jennings III. Hay's face alit as if ten thousand lights reflected there.

"He's so tiny, Justine; just like you!"

"Hay! Give me the baby. He won't break."

He rarely left the room; just sat for hours marveling at the little bundle nestled closely to me.

"Now you have someone else to spoil; just as you've spoiled me," I say watching him cradle the baby.

"Oh, yeah! I'm on a mission to super-spoil my clan!"

****

Months became years, and we soon welcomed our little smiling Harrison.

"He's so bright! Look at him smile!"

Both Carla and Bev chorused: "Gas pains!"

Time has flown, zoomed by and I am now bombarded with sweat socks, tennis, athletic equipment, balls, bikes, motorized cars, sports games and super jock activities! They both have morphed into Hay, fully equipped with his mannerisms. "Man sharpens man..." They are their Father's sons.

We are not in a "fairy-tale"; though much of our lives have unfolded in storybook fashion. Our lives are complex. I pray daily that our joy doesn't end. Hay used to say this when we'd visit the Tisdales and their brood. Complete.

"I call it complete," he said with wishful thinking.

The Chinaberry Tree

His wishes have come true. We are a complete family now. Elation is my constant companion. Thanking God Almighty for continual favor and blessings is a daily event for me; for us. The ups and downs in life are effectively handled; we have shared parenting. When Hay speaks; we all listen. He's just that commanding!

I have concluded: God knew just what both he and I needed. Our season of change was orchestrated by Him. He knows our beginning; He sees our end. We are now rearing "Little Mighty Men of Valor" just like Haywood. These "apples" hang out a lot with this "tree".

My continual praise and thankfulness is offered everyday. I let God know just how grateful I am. It's like brushing my teeth, combing my hair, bathing, feeding my family; I just must do it well and often. In this state of awareness I have never been happier. I have taken to mothering, just as astutely as I took to writing. It's all second nature.

The Chinaberry Tree

LOVE IN THE

ULTIMATE ARENA

FEBRUARY 15, 2008

The Chinaberry Tree

The writings, a strong scrawl with a firmly gripped pen. There it lay naked and exposed on Hay's massive Sligh desk. Curious, I picked it up and began to read; tidying his area momentarily forgotten.

"If you've ever been in love, then you truly understand that love is wonderful; grand in its truest sense. Love is sanctioned by God I Am Himself; for He is Love. Love is the answer to all the uncertainties in life. "Love vaunteth not its self; is not puffed up." We are admonished to, "love ye one another; just as God loved the World, he gave his only begotten Son; that whosoever believes on him shall have everlasting life." Through this grand unselfish act God and man reconciled.

Everlasting life is free. Son Supreme Jesus is the epitome of God's love; a show of His love for his creation. Let love abound freely. God keeps us from all danger; the way a great father covers his sons; his offspring. Lord, my growing offspring are covered!

I shall always reach out to you, knowing you wait to hear my call. So I answer your 'clarion call'; I am willing to walk with you all the way. Show me your plan for me. I accept this call on my life. I am a man complete, ready to give my all to thee. You admonished me to come on up a little higher. So I bow down, praise, worship and accept thee wholly!

Higher! Higher, now! I'm going higher in thee! Where is that place that is a respite for my soul? Show me; teach me; mold me, Light of My Life! Show me the roadmap to Heaven. 'Heaven is a place I want to be!"

Clear and sharp, meant personally for him. "The Clarion call," I softly mouth as Hay's letter to God flutters back to the desk. I knew. I've always known him as a devout man of God. He did not take advantage of me. He has the heart and soul of a minister. I trust his every inclination. Haywood's told me numerous

The Chinaberry Tree

times his Uncle spoke this on his life. I often call him "Brother Minister." Hay is answering God. He's put it in writing.

"Write the vision; make it plain; that he may run that readeth it; and not faint. For the vision is only for a while; it shall speak and not lie." Habakuk Three fits perfectly with what Hay's done. The vision of winning souls for Christ has been there all the time.

"They call me 'Deacon' cause I always carry my Bible and pray before games," He's shared.

"Will you pray for us, Haywood?" I have asked sensing his oneness with God; knowing that what's happened God did it. He hangs out often with Pastor Dr. Sloan. I now wonder if he's teaching Hay, helping him answer "Walking Up the King's Highway: none can walk up there but the pure in heart."
At first I thought it was Hay's celebrity that made our leader call on him. I now conclude "he's teaching Hay."

"We shall know each other by our love."

"Stay in service," Sloan exclaims. We are present and accounted for; never late.

"O God, My God; you're not a game; but Haywood is now chasing You. Will you acknowledge this; turn and receive him?" I ponder as I finish cleaning Hay's study. We have much help, but only I am admitted to this spacious inner sanctum. He is surrounded by books, ledgers, printouts, computers, et al the needs to manage his many interests. I replace each object to place, then exit and close the door.

****

So I await just one more grand announcement. My Hay is an extraordinary man comfortably existing in ordinary arenas. He's still Athletic Director, coaching varsity. He handles all. I marvel at his perseverance. It is night. His game

The Chinaberry Tree

watching over. I depart the den to begin my nightly beauty regimen. After a time I sense his presence.

"What's that smell? It has the aroma of cherry blossoms. There is a Chinese belief that 'if one is under fragrant cherry blossoms you must embrace, as if honoring their offering;' not only beauty, but the fragrant aroma."

"It's mom's favorite lotion. She smelled of it every day of her life. I use it because it's like extending a part of her. I think of her as nearby."

"I love cherry blossom, Justine. I love you, so the lotion is my favorite as well. May I?"

Hay took the bottle from my hand and poured some in his palms, rubbed them together, then smoothed the unguent over my shoulders and upper arms. I was lulled and quickened by his touch.

"Don't start nothing'; won't be nothing'!" I said with less bravado. I didn't mind one iota if Mt. St. Helen exploded in our bedroom in extreme pyroclastic clouds; and we float away together.

"Come to me, Jus!" He requested.

"The boys...," I protested.

"...Are two rooms away."

"Love you so much, Hay!"

"Love you more," he answers and I take his hand.

My beloved is mine; and I am his. It's our indelible "Yin-Yang" experience.

****

Hay gets lost in me; as well as in play with our two little pistols. I watch them in the beginning play of touch football. Guy stuff abounds. Guffaws, hoots, and loud squeals fill the air. Young Hay replicates his father's actions. Harrison is toddling right along. He cries in frustration at missing the ball.

The Chinaberry Tree

"What shall I do with the 'boo-hoo baby'?" Young Hay asks as Harrison pouts and whines.

He stamps his little foot and says, "Na-a-ah!"

"Boo-hoo!" Young Hay repeats. Harrison goes over and slugs young Hay.

"Oh, whoa! Harrison, play fair. No hitting! It's okay to feel disappointed, but don't hit because you feel that way." Hay instructed firmly.

"This is tag; not tackle. Touch not hitting, okay?"

"But dad they hit harder in those games we watch."

"Look, guy! Those are seasoned tough guys. What are they called?"

"Pros."

"Exactly. You guys are just learning. Play fair."

"Oh, awright, Dad!"

"Young Hay, take it easy; don't heckle. His limbs are not quite developed as yours. Cut your brother some slack, okay?"

"Of course, Dad. Come on Harrison. I'll show you how to catch. Here goes the snap; come and get it!"

Harrison ran fast, young Hay got closer before the toss. It was a gentle toss. Harrison caught it, a big grin on his face. Hay joined me on the patio.

"Pray we get it right, hon!"

"Oh, we're okay; doing fine with this parenting thing! We're all in good hands."

Mel's twin Jacob arrived and joined the boys in the yard.

"You getting' dressed for the Sweetheart Bash?"

"Yep. Duty calls," I answered.

****

The multi-purpose room of Sloan Ministries Perfecting Church overflowed. The "Sweetheart Social" was a plan to get Christian couples to

The Chinaberry Tree

socialize and fraternize from seven until eleven PM. Pastor Fred Sloan and Lady Mildred greeted us warmly, then invited us to enjoy a sumptuous buffet and dance.

"Fellows, its all right to dance with your wife. Enjoy!" He offered, then led the head table to the buffet. We relaxed and visited many tables of eight. The crowd looked like a multi-petaled flower of pink and white. We took leave just before eleven and ran into the Sloans departing also.

"Must get home to our 'ones," Hay said leading us to make a "beeline" to the Bentley. They looked at each other and grinned broadly.

"That was very nice!"

"He does everything in a big way."

"Was it better than our mall date?"

"No. Not really. Can you believe it's been over six years?"

"Time does fly, filled with great events!"

"Too tired, my lovely?"

"Lately I feel kinda' icky."

"Look I'll drop you; take Jake home. You turn in, get some rest."

"It's a deal," I said dispelling the squeamish feeling I had.

Twenty minutes later I was in bed, covers up to my ears, hoping a little rest would help.

The Chinaberry Tree

****

Delivering Jacob home took only a matter of minutes. I toss my keys on a ring in the kitchen; soon hurrying to get ready for bed just to be near her. She is snoring softly sleeping soundly. I soon hold her closely. All is well in my world. It occurs to me Justine is with child. I'm soon thinking, ruminating that it's a girl.

Justine and I are one. God is not hanging out in our bedroom. We are admonished "to be fruitful and multiply." God did not say He'd be hanging about. I'm elated God sees us as He does. I am "at home" in this moment. The fact that almonds adds to the effect. Trust from my fruit; in "leaps and bounds" keeps on growing!

BLOSSOMS OR BERRIES

PART II

The Chinaberry Tree

Haywood is a planner. He makes plans, then sets out to bring them to fruition. So long ago he'd planned to get us together. That led to our great marriage. Devoted. He just doesn't quit; never dissuaded. Our home he designed and built is beautiful. When we'd returned from our glorious honeymoon planners and excavators, pourers and builders were fast at work; putting his plan into action. Terraced yards were planed, planted, and Hay ordered numerous fruit trees, shrubbery, and two saplings from China. The pictures were beautiful. Cherry blossoms were bountiful, pinkish white with ruby red centers. The chinaberry tree in bloom with purplish flowers was tall and stately, offering much shade. Still I had reservations about that tree. Another genus had yellowish golden flowers, and orangey brown clusters of berries. Beware its odiferous nature. Bitter and sweet. It's first bloom engaged the onlooker. It's later stage of growth gave off a stinky odiferous smell; plus the berries were poisonous, and only palatable to fowl and some birds species.

Our terrace garden resembled a huge cross. Shrubbery surrounded the exterior planes. Garden shrubbery is cut and shaved, sheared, then flat and rounded in uniform shapes. Hay was speaking to the gardener. I stood nearby, picking up bits and pieces of the conversation. The gardener soon left. I took the moment to inquire.

"Hay, why these two geneses of the Chinaberry Tree?" He didn't answer right away, so I posed another question.

"When did you visit China?

"Didn't have to, Justine. I know these types to be stately sturdy, have great purple flowers, or golden ones; and will provide shade for summer."

He left me to speak briefly to the planers. He is unnerved.

"Build a terrace around the Chinaberry. It molts berries. We'll clear them away from time to time. They easily sprout. If we don't clear them others may

The Chinaberry Tree

sprout."

"Sounds like a lot of trouble, Mr. Jennings! I've been meaning to speak with you about those Chinaberries. They're more indigenous to the Southeast."

"How well I know! Indulge me! Can we make it work?" Hay asked retreating to join me.

He said little else; so I let it go. We walked about our land. He'd ordered white Magnolias. Gates were being erected. We walked the extent. Hay seemed disquieted. I know he's concerned; thinking it through.

"Our children will take full advantage of our land," he began.

"I can see that also." We soon sat for a time on the patio.

"You think I've been trying to replicate Uncle Joe's farm? Am I trying to bring the Southeast and set it smack dab in the Midwest?"

"What do you think, Hay?" I wonder who he's mimicking when he used "smack-dab"?

"Be back soon," he says then heads for his study.

A soft breeze lulls me into complacency. I yawn, rise, and start for bed. Near his study bay window I stop momentarily. He is praying. Audibly the petition goes forth. He is bowed. I also lower my head in total agreement of all he asks. He will work it all out. Perhaps if we rest on it; decide tomorrow.

"Strong faith-filled men can handle much," He has shared often enough. I have seen him encounter someone he's not seen in a while. Later he prays for them. He's not ashamed to offer a "hue and cry" on highway or byway, whenever it's required of him. "True and abiding" is what he's been. No "sad shores of loneliness" for us. He keeps on lifting many up in prayer. God is up to something. Moments later I enter our home and stop at his study. Ideas will come after we rest. It shall be worked out.

"Much on your mind?"

The Chinaberry Tree

"Quite a bit, My Little Woman; but I'll be on soon. Save some room for me!"

****

"Whatever will be; will be; que sera; sera!" I conclude as I fall; am slipping into sleep. The cool air and warm sun, then a warm bath have set the tone for dreamland. The next morn I forged ahead; broached the subject before he did.

"Hon, I love cherries. Let's settle for fruit trees, especially cherries. As an accolade to my Mom? They will be beautiful, smell wonderful like the lotion you help me spread all over me."

"Cherries and almonds; it reminds me of both." I continued intent on changing his mind about Chinaberries."

"We can harvest cherries, share with family and friends; make jellies; and I might even try making cherry wine."

"It's a thought, Little Woman." Mac has even tried to dissuade me from even ordering the Chinaberries."

"Did he say why?"

"The berries rot the ground; not fit for any animal; could be poisonous to our children. All great reasons. I'm beginning to see his point. You don't want them either?"

"No. I love fruit we can eat. Cherries and oranges we can eat." He smiled that nervous wry smile playing at the corners of his mouth; most appealing to me."

"You keep me grounded. It's a deal! I'll tell Mac to order two cherry trees instead."

"We can always visit Aunt Carrie and Ferndale on the farm."

"That we can! Very soon, Jus'! So much has happened in the south; I've put our trip off many times."

The Chinaberry Tree

"We will go. You've told me often enough it's your beginning. You were quite fond of him. He spoke great things on your life; like a mentor or father figure would."

"That he did! We travelled south every summer. Mother rounded us up; then we were on our way!"

"What a multi-faceted life you've lead!"

"It was paradise! Mom often says a change came with the intervention of all those casinos. Places that used to be grounded in Christian faith, farming and mercantile. Now casinos have sprung up all over." He frowned furrowing his brow.

"Paradise has changed; sometimes not for the better. Droughts, ravaging storms, erosion, and unrest replaced simple living. Inspite of all that, my heart still beckons me to Joe Love's Farm. You've got to see it to believe it!"

"I believe you, Hay! I know you. You'll go forth in hope and faith. I want to see what's calling you back south. I want to put faces with those southern drawls over the phone."

Sitting under that tree with Unc, Ferndale, Aunt Carrie, Eliza, and a whole bunch of relatives, early morns, and late evening, became our sharing times. Drunken guinea fowl lurched about after ingesting those chinaberries. We laughed."

"Uncle Joe had strong faith and taught a purposeful life to all who'd listen."

"Yes, Jus! Love of family, and living right; ever thankful of all the Lord provided. So much is coming back to me. You surely listened well, my girl!"

"We'll go soon?"

"Very soon, my Lil' Woman!"

"Stop calling me that!"

The Chinaberry Tree

"We are all 'trees'. I've heard you call us 'trees'! It is true! I can see why you think of us as 'trees' Shorty!"

"Well, now! I'm Magpie, Lil' Woman, and now Shorty?"

"No. You're the half of me; the love of my life."

"Soft-soaper!"

"Jus', I'm trying to get past the name-calling!"

"Come on. Look in the book with me again. Let's see you remember."

He opened a picture book; and I began. "This is Fern-Dale, loves his golden Palamino, long salt n' pepper hair, Aunt Carrie there is the originator of the best lemonade ever made. Has her own secret recipe. That's Willy and Abraham Dale's children. Eliza, Carrie's younger sister. Your mother, Father Haywood, Mel, Beverly and the twins." We ogled the photos peering closely.

"Hay you have a fine family!" I complimented.

The pictures of extensive land, planted acreages, a huge pond; cars parked near a sloped incline, leading to the main farmhouse; a large corral with three other horses; and more candid photos. A man of his word, I knew we were going when Hay bought the van.

"Anyone ready to hit the road?" He'd asked sheepishly.

We nodded in the affirmative. I fully realize it's most important to him. Hay craves the connection of his past to our future. He fully wants to connect us.

THE CHINABERRY TREE

PART III

The Chinaberry Tree

A fine mist hung in the air. Leaves were covered with crystallized beads of moisture. It is my morning constitutional trek across the expanse of land I'd bought for our home. These varied walks help me take stock in all My God has gifted me. Briefly I glance back at the home I'd built for Justine. It is special and palatial; more warm and homey than the St. Pete's mansion I'd sold. I wanted her with me. Loved her so long. It was hard to harness such feelings. I kept busy. She was what was missing in St. Pete's and my life.

The age old brown parka I keep because her first touch is upon it. I lift the collar. The crisp morning air is nippy from the season's change. Cold air has met warm air and I brush moisture now collecting on my jacket.

Getting up early, removing myself from the soft sweet scent of her, and trekking through these woods tears me away from her overwhelming beauty. I don't want her to have my soul; but anything is hers if she asks me. I am lost in her. The grand design of my God has made all I've planned unfold valiantly. I've honored God, honored her, and Uncle Joseph Love.

The clear concise still small voice within me has prompted me to "come on up a little higher"; and I am answering; embracing it; living it. I have pursued God without reservations; as I have pursued Justine. Almost eight months of dating and just being with her changed her solemnity to glee. Tenacity won her over.
She kept saying: "Mr. Bon vivant, you can have anyone you like!" Then I'd answer: "I came back for you, Jus'! It's you I need!"

She'd gaze up at me like I was "Too Tall Jones"; I did not relent or waver in my purpose. We kissed like we were still in high school. I soon figured it out. She was virginal and untouched.

"God, you saved her for me!" I held back; though I wanted to give her much of my wealth. Loved the way she looked, all bright-eyed, full of joy when

The Chinaberry Tree

I'd gifted her 'baubles, bangles, and gems'. Even when I told her all; she continued acting as if it didn't matter. I am so excited when she submits to me.

The level place comes into view, a bluff over looking the valley. It is more breathtaking than any chalet, chateau, Casa, Castle, or Hacienda we've encountered in our travels.

We have just one more place to visit. I suspect she'll like it better than when we pay a visit to my franchises. It is an indelible part of my past. Be with us Jesus; be with us Lord!"

I keep mulling over what must be. Still I've put it off numerous times. What is different? Mom always got us on the move. Dad could take it or leave it. In-laws. Was he fed up with all those in-laws? Never said but moved slowly.

****

Duty always seemed to be calling. There is much to manage. So I shoulder the responsibility, putting nothing on Jus'. It's just my way. I'd been honed by real men; men who took the reins, took charge, til all is handled. Jus' is the woman I've always wanted; to love, to care for. All others faded into obscurity. It's not just her beauty. She's so intellectual, quick minded, and she's a wonderful homemaker and mother. Wow! She's all I need in this world! Yet there are times I distance myself before she fully takes me over.

During high school I'd dated Betty Deer briefly. We only went out a few times. We became friends. Melvin was my "sounding board". I'd confided much to him.

"I saw her today, Mel, and waved," I'd report.

"Why don't you ask her out?" He'd inquired.

"I've thought of that. She makes me tongue-tied, Mel!"

"Well, it won't happen, Hay, if you don't do the 'guy thing'!?"

"What 'guy-thing'?"

The Chinaberry Tree

"Take the initiative, sap!"

"Stop calling me that!"

"Ask her out, Hay!" He'd advised.

A few times I was brave. She'd been giddy about our wins; dominating our brief encounter. I'd said exactly two words to her.

"Keep on winning, Haywood!" She'd ended.

"Okay, Justine," I'd answered even more tongue-tied. Getting a date with her then seemed hopeless.

Betty Deer has returned to Sullivan, now a career woman personified. I sense "green lights" flashing all around; my systems say "no"! So I befriend her and sidestep everyone. She's very beautiful flipping her cascade of hair, now expertly groomed, those endless pigtails and braids all gone.

"Too late!" I think and go on past her 'come and get it' attitude. Sometimes I think of Betty as the prevailing weed of the Southeast; it does not quit; won't stop covering much territory. Betty always has something to discuss with me. I allow her to go on and on. She retreats after a while. Another day she's back again with a whole flurry of interesting ideas with which to engage me.

Betty is like the "node" on Kudzu's running vine. Her interest re-grows and begins again though we're discussing school interests. Her "mile-a-minute" conversations seem to grow "a foot-a-nite".

Never one to harm anyone; I listen, am friendlier and encourage her in her brilliant ideas. I do show her I'm a "one woman man". I have given her the many "pejorative" nicknames of Kudzu, because her attempts have not ceased.

Like Kudzu, Betty has many positive uses. She is salve for our failing test scores. Her initiated "fast forward program" for our students is a grand success at every level. "Dr. Betty Deer, I salute you!"

The Chinaberry Tree

I do not wish to classify Betty as rejectable. She is very beautiful. We include her in our "circle of interest"; and I invite a few more single colleagues to our gatherings. Am I a match-maker? Oh contraire, just allowing her to consider greener pastures. So I pray for one and all in my circle.

Most Holy Blessed Lord, please protect us from eave to eave, door to door, house to home; on highway, byway, even airways. We are many and we travel here and there. Please send mighty angels before us. In Heaven, on earth, even unto eternity; I request Justine, My great Lil Woman at my side. Forever graciously thankful for all on loan to me. It's your son, Haywood Jennings, Jr. Man of You, Personified ever faithful. Amen.

As far as the eye can see it is beautiful. For a time I stand then start back for our home. I am a great steward o'er all.

The Chinaberry Tree

LOVE IN THE ULTIMATE ARENA

BOOK III

The Chinaberry Tree

Grogginess made me weigh whether to go to church. The morning after the "sweetheart social" finds me much out of it. I rose with trepidation and made my way to the table. Hay and the boys were eating a light breakfast of waffles and juice. I greeted them and made tea and toast. Triplets, they were dressed in tailored suits; napkins at their necks to defray crumbs and such.

"You three are very handsome," I complimented; then took a bite of toast and a sip of tea. The flutters in my stomach increased.

"Oh! Wow! I must have been hungry!" Three pairs of eyes stared at me.

"You look kinda peeked. You wanna stay home?"

"Wouldn't miss it for the world! Nope." A few more bites I returned to our room to get dressed.

"I feel pregnant." I soon changed suits thrice; my waistbands kinda tight.

"I hope it's a girl," I thought joining them a half hour later.

****

A hush fell over the worshippers as we entered the outer court of Sloan's Self-Perfecting Sanctuary. We were soon seated. The crescendo of rolling drums, tinkling cymbals, string and harps, even horns accompanied an electronic melodeon playing a familiar inspiration.

"Let the praise begin!" The Reverend Doctor Fred Sloan announced. Thousands rose up to welcome the presence of our Savior Devine.

"In the beauty of the Spirit, I welcome you in this place! He is here! Come let us worship Him! Come on join in and welcome our Lord Jesus in the beauty of holiness!"

The Chinaberry Tree

Enthused and animated we join the Jubilee Praise Team singing with fervor, It's in your praise!" All around hope filled worshippers peered skyward and sang on one accord.

"All the glory, honor, and praise belongs to our God!

Lord, we worship you!

For all you've done

Sent Us Jesus, Thy Darling Son;

Because he paid it

Our victory is won!

We worship and adore you, Majesty!

You are our all n' all!

Hallelujah! Hallelujah! Glory"

As one melodious song of praise ended, another began.

"Jehovah, Jireh, My Provider

Jehovah Nisi, Lord you reign in

Victory; Jehovah Shalom,

You're my Prince of Peace;

And I worship you because

Of who you are..."

The Chinaberry Tree

It was abject praise; love sung in our ultimate arena; all on one accord. How glorious is the joyful sound! Harrison clapped his tiny hands. Hay picked him up. Harrison stared at Hay's closed eyes; then mimicked him. They were triplets singing praise to our God! The flutters began again. I took Haywood's hand and placed it on my stomach. The rippling movements of life did not cease. Briefly he opened his eyes.

"I hope it's a girl," I whispered.

Pastor Sloan was speaking once more.

"Oh to be kept by Jesus!

 Oh the joy of my soul;

 Like the sea billows roll;

 Since Jesus came into my heart…"

I could feel His presence all around us. A third child, a girl for me. I am elated!

"We worship your Holy Ways, O God!"

****

The service flowed freely in the auspices of God's Grace. Soon Pastor Sloan lead us to the very end.

"Welcome Saints! Praise His name in this place! Our hearts and minds are on our Savior Divine, Yeshua, Our Deliverer from the Royal Priesthood of Melchizedec is surely among us. There are so many names for Jesus, that Perfect Lamb that was slain for you and me. INRE, once for all He gave us the victory over sin and death. Which is that 'second death'. You oughta run willy nilly and snatch many from the gaping abyss of hell's fire." The worship ebbed and flowed for a time. He took time to praise our God.

"Lady Mildred, would you stand? Come. Fellows, Men of God, it's all right to bestow due benevolence on your wife." He embraced her as she drew near to him.

"If you don't love your wife, who on earth you gonna love? Lady Mildred is fairer than Saraii at sixty-two. I'd be willing to box with Jehosphat for her hand?"

Warm responses, "Hallelujah!"

"Our 'Sweetheart' gathering last evening was marvelous! Trustee Larry Wilson, and Brother Reggie Carter were makin' some smooth moves on the floor. Oh, yes! Hang on to your hats now! Minister Haywood Jennings among others was carryin' on with the missus also! What a grand time we had!" Applause ensued.

"Hang on Sloopy! Hang on! Lady Mildred was lookin' so goood! We had to go home earrrrrly!" The delivery was trite light wit!

"Would the planning committee please stand?" Twenty parishioners stood; the applause deafening.

"Thank you, sowers, good stewards of faith. Now let us get into some Word!"

Lady Mildred stepped forth and read the scripture emblazoned on three mega-screens.

The Chinaberry Tree

"Please turn with me to II Chronicles: Chapter 6: 24-25. Stand and be heard by the glory of God!"

We responded then rose, and stood up in honor.

"If my people have sinned against you, humble themselves and pray; confess Your Name; turn from unrighteousness, and make supplication; then you will hear from Heaven; forgive their sins; and bring them back to the land which was given to them, and their fathers. May God truly bless this edifying word as it goes forth!" She ended and returned to her seat at the "right hand" of Sloan.

The exogeus in his mind; he stood tall and stepped to the podium. A soul-stirring impartation ensued.

"What a joy we have under the anointing! The 'anointing oil' destroys the yoke! So says Moses in Deuteronomy Thirteen. We are standing, resting, working and honoring God in the midst of glory. Ain't no scatterin' and shatterin' up in here! For you are the Lord's sheep on loan to me. I am happy to set this tone, lead and guide you to right-living; as a chosen tender of God's flock it's my aim to keep you safely in the fold. Greener pastures, to me are the gates of Heaven. Ain't no landlords up there! There is room for us all! Jesus has said, 'there are many mansions'. If it were not so; I would have told you. There are twelve gates of single pearls each. Streets are paved with gold. None. None. None can walk up there but the repentant pure in heart! We'll be walking up the King's Highway! Flowing rivers on both sides; trees of life full of fruit! Hallelujah! Hallelujah!"

He sang melodically:

"This is Holy Ground!

This is Holy Ground!

The Chinaberry Tree

So come and bow, bow down..."

Cherabim! Seraphim and

Choirs encamp around, sing around, and

worship around God's Throne!"

"Holy! Holy! Holy! Thou art Holy!

They are not under the constraints of time! We have marked off time; Put ourselves on a time table. Didn't you read? Haven't you heard a day to our God is as a thousand years? Hallelujah! God is so grand, so Omnipresent He sits outside time. He knows our beginnings; and He sees our ends. A day in the courts of our God is better than a thousand elsewhere! Hallelujah! Hallelujah! Be careful what you ask for, what you hope for. For if you remain in the Spirit, in oneness with God He will give you the very desires of your heart.

This word I give to the weary. Don't get weary in doing well. Let me encourage you today. "Eyes have not seen; ears have not heard, nor hearts felt what God has in store for those that love Him.

To know Him is to love Him!

To know Him is to fear Him

To fear Him is to keep His principles!"

Did you hear me? God wants us to fear Him and keep His statutes! Let me encourage you on your way. The natural man needs to come on up a little higher, seek His face, turn from wickedness, create a wonderful relationship with Him. If you are rebellious and stiff-necked you go on out in your own way. Messin' up, giving up, forgetting covenants, and doing your own thing.

The Chinaberry Tree

Don't you need a closer walk with Him? Don't you need to turn around and tell Him all about your troubles? He will. He will. God is tender in mercy. He will hear your fervent cry; answer you by and by!

Is your prayer-wheel turning? Is God's fire burning in your life? Come on up a little higher! Lay all your skirmishes in life at His feet! Fear not. Resist not his intervention. He is a problem-solver. There is nothing too hard for the one that neither slumbers or sleeps! Hallelujah! The signs of times are here, there, everywhere! Wars, somebody's talking about wars; the crazed are building bigger bombs that will annihilate not only the world, but the crafter also. Strong storms are raging ravaging the states. Fires, rumbles and trembling are happening all over the globe! Our children need Jesus. Help Lord Jesus! Don't you be shaken! Trust! Trust and never doubt. He surely will bring you out of every calamity! Lean on Him! He shall pass over his people. In all this destruction; He'll pass over his people." He leaned forward.

"Hear me, Saints of God! O' new Israelites, mark your sign over the doorpost. The Saints shall not be shaken or broken! Repent all that is past; fall down, fall down on your knees; crying Lord, have mercy please; and He shall give you victory over all your trials. King Solomon says in Chronicles 6:24-25:

"For it is written, if my people have sinned against you, humble themselves and pray; confess your name; turn from wickedness; humble and pray, then you, O' God will hear from Heaven and forgive their sins, and bring them back to the land you have given them and their fathers. America is also such a place; founded on 'In God We Trust' How many of us are steeped in wickedness; and stopped trusting God? 'Give me your tired, your hungry, your persecuted, yearning to be free..."

The Chinaberry Tree

All masses are comin' to America! Home of the free, and the brave. They've come trod upon, stolen, bought, indentured; many have come. Our God sets free the captives; be that Israelites or slaves brought in the bowels of rancid ships. Our God sets free.

"Turn from wickedness; seek His face; trust him; all you have to do is trust Him. Hallelujah! Hallelujah! The doors to this glorious temple swing wide to welcome you. Won't you come, right now?" Hundreds joined a 'sure foundation' a glorious throne room; and he welcomed all. Fred Sloan is 'man sharpening men.'

****

My meeting with Dr. Fred Sloan was progressing well. No stone unturned, he'd began to hold classes for three of us. Pastor Sloan had taught six years at our local seminary. Short cut. Didn't give it one thought. We were being groomed for his ministry.

Our class had begun six months ago, after each met with him privately. He'd offered tea and scotch butter cookies. He handed me a tin to take to Jus' and our boys. Awkward? At first he'd given me an account of his initial calling. "Let me begin, Minister Haywood by quoting Proverbs 37:17, a familiar scripture touted often among laymen. It states:

"As iron sharpens iron, so one man sharpens another.' Look at the word 'countenance'. It is now my job to approve and support your efforts. I will also counsel you and offer advice from time to time. One of your greatest attributes I've made note of is you are humbled before God. This makes my work with you easy.

You see my brother, you are an extraordinary man. Being a famous ball-player did not make you lose yourself. Being rich has not bored you. As you began

The Chinaberry Tree

to bring your wonderful family to Sloan's I was happy in my spirit. When you spoke, took on tasks you performed quite admirably, there was a glow about you.

'Iron sharpens iron; man sharpens the countenance of his friend.'

Minister Haywood, you were ready long ago when you answered the proverbial clarion call. You know God's voice. I can see it changed your very life!" He paused. I took the opportunity to speak.

"There is a huge farm in southeast Mississippi. My mother spirited us there every summer. Soon as school was out she gathered us, cajoled my father, and we were off to visit great Uncle Joseph Love. I was just a young sprout when he began to speak on my life. He told me I'd be a great man, especially a great man of God. What happened when you heard 'the clarion call'; Dr. Fred?"

"Why, what most of us do when we get it and we stew in unreadiness; I ran from it!"

"I chose pro-ball; what did you choose instead?"

"I told myself I could still be a 'good man', a scientist. I wanted to study his whole creation. So I headed for the University's halls of higher learning."

"A little stop-off in the world?"

"So to speak; but not completely. Whatever I undertook I left the worldly ideals behind to hone those studies."

"Grounded. You were grounded."

"That's astute of you, Haywood! Exactly. I'd almost earned my doctorate. One late night; I'd studied all day; was kind of out of it. Somehow I took the wrong turn. The streets around the college were like a maze. I thought I knew them

The Chinaberry Tree

well, but somehow I missed my turn; I took another thinking it would lead me back to my street. Suddenly there was a tall figure in my path. I swerved to miss him just barely. I went a ways further. I looked back quickly he was gone. After a beat I inched forward and there he stood. If you asked me to describe him other than his bright eyes, I cannot. 'Are you lost, brother?' He'd asked."

"Are *you* lost?" I'd asked repeating his question. I looked about, not a car in sight, but I was on a 'one-way' street.

"It was a metaphor, Haywood! I was getting a doctorate in the sciences. God wanted me to obtain a doctorate in the study of Him. This is so powerful! The man was gone; but my realizations remained. God was calling me to a higher level in him. He protected me on that road. No cars came. I made my way back. The traveler was put there to turn me around. Brother Minister, I turned around!"

"Let me tell you, Dr. Sloan; God does not do anything the same way twice. I feel him in, on, all around me. He leads me, orchestrates my very life. His call to me was as clear and concise as the sound of a struck gong. I was dreaming I was dreaming one night after my second injury. At first I thought it was the pain meds; but I was wide awake. The image of Uncle Joe had awakened me. My eyes were riveted on him. He was singing to me, a well known powerful rendition we'd sang at Rocky Point Church.

> "Zion is calling you
>
> To a higher place of praise!
>
> To stand upon the mountain
>
> And magnify his name

The Chinaberry Tree

Tell all the people,

Every nation that He reigns!

Zion is calling you

To a higher place of praise!

"Haywood!" He continued.

"He's calling you, boy! Just like I told you! Be brave! Take up the staff! Come on into the camp, Haywood!"

"That's what struck me. He never called me Haywood. Referred to me as Godwin; said with God I can always win." He faded. Yet there was a peace in that hospital room. I was alone, but God was there!"

"This is so powerful, Brother Minister. Consider yourself being sharpened! Welcome to the staff of Sloan's Perfecting Church. We welcome you in the spirit of the Living God. You shall catch many souls! Lift the Savior up!"

We embraced. Another level of commitment had begun. I am truly complete.

****

Pastor Fred is travelling often; leaving matters in the hands of his son Andrew and three of the ministerial staff. The Bahamas beckon he and Lady Mildred. They soon set off six months later attended by a whole bevy of "armor bearers". My Hay was chosen to bring the message the next hot July service. Time is winding up; and our blessings grew in 'leaps and bounds'.

The Chinaberry Tree

Haywood projects a commanding presence. Service was more than routine. Hay's chosen exogeous was "Perfection In Christ".

First he posed a question: "How do we reach true perfection? Is it top of the world, with worldly gain? Do we 'fine tune' our minds? How about a well toned body, with six and eight-packs galore? Do we shave pounds off our robust frame? It's not about all that! What really counts is you don't have to look perfect to be perfected in Christ! No! You don't have to be perfect to choose a life well-melded in Jesus! Come as you are! Spots, wrinkles, and all.

I am reminded of David out tending sheep. They wandered through thistle and thicket. David annihilated a ferocious lion, an angry bear. David was in the midst of dirt, grime. Even the sheep's wool was tufted, matted and dirty. Oh but when he sheared off an inch or so those sheep were whiter than snow.

Don't you want to be whiter than snow? When Jesus shears away your sins; though they be crimson, scarlet, you, too are white as snow! You'd better say 'Amen' right here! Why don't you add three 'Hallelujahs'? Let us explore here our greatest perfection in Christ. Only he who knew no sin could save and raise us!

When you're admonished to forgive all, no matter the slight; He wants to take you higher in Him! Hallelujah!

There's another 'Patron of Perfection': Enoch loved God, walked with Him; and talked with Him along 'the narrow way'; that road less travelled. It's hot near the flame of God! Enoch got close to the 'unapproachable light' of God. He became God's 'friend'. Just like Israel 'God knew his name'! After a fruitful life Enoch was translated up in Heaven.

The Chinaberry Tree

In writings by, M.J. Abydie: Enoch was taught by angels; wrote books, Enoch I, Enoch II, and III. In this compilation Abydie concurred Enoch holds a high seat in Heaven. Can you imagine getting so perfectly close to God you don't taste death; but are brought right up into Heaven?"

"Hallelujah! Save us, Lord!" an elder cried. Worshippers rose; Haywood stepped it up.

"God stopped time for another Patron perfect for His purpose. Abrahm dwelled among his people for seventy-five years, along with his wife Sarai of sixty-two years. God called them out to the Land of Canaan. Abrahm was not perfect, but he was perfect for God's purpose. On this journey Abrahm gained wealth. Jerohabim, King of Egypt sought out after Sarai, who was most fair. Sixty-two. What does a woman look like at sixty-two?

I have an Aunt Carrie who is sixty two. She doesn't look a day over forty. When you're favored of God you are a new creature; there's a glow to your countenance, a lilt in your step, a gleam in your eye. God stopped time for Sarai. He'd promised Abrahm he'd be the Father of Many Nations. Sarai was barren and Abrahm was old in years. They were not perfect, but they were perfect for God's purpose. They gained wealth; they gained a promise from God. In obeying God, he looked out for them. They ultimately gained a 'name change'. Abraham and Sarah became the parents of many nations. By the God of Abraham, HEI VAV HEI YUD. He is the covenant-keeper! He keeps His word, cannot lie!"

How can we not explore the life of Moses, the writer of the Pentitude; the first five books of the Bible. Moses is the greatest prophet ever known; a true shepherd who led the Israelites from slavery in Egypt; the only human to see the face of God. No man can stand to look upon His Glory!

The Chinaberry Tree

Moses cried out: 'Lord, please show me your glory!' God, in his unapproachable light' passes nearby and Moses glimpses the 'backside' of God! Hallelujah! Shout Halelujah! Moses was not perfect. He had a speech problem. In anger he slew one of Pharoahs guards for beating a slave woman. After freeing the Israelites while wandering the people became thirsty. There at Meribah he smote the rock angrily; and water gushed forth. Moses was not perfect; but he was truly perfect for what God had in mind!"

Are you perfect? God has said 'all have sinned and come short of His glory!' I am not perfect; but he chose me for a purpose. I-I-I don't know about you, but I'm going to step out on faith. Seek His Holy Face! Come on up a little higher. Grace abounds in Him! Will you answer Him today in your perfection?

Can you answer His call:

    a. David answered

    b. Enoch answered

    c. Abraham answered

    d. Moses answered

When he calls you will you answer? Will you cast all your cares on Him because He cares for you; I am hopeful of that promise in Psalms 1:6: My children's children shall be blessed. There's none perfect; no not one; but you can be perfect for God's plan in your life. Won't you come? The doors to this Perfecting Temple welcome you! Come on into the Throne Room!"

The Chinaberry Tree

Many forged forward. Hay ascended the four tiered steps; standing among the crowd shaking many hands. We are caught up in redemptive praise. Minister Andrew stepped to the podium. We joined him in song:

> "Consuming fire!
>
> Sweet perfume; your
>
> Awesome spirit fills
>
> This room…
>
> This is Holy Ground!"

James 4:8 beckons us too:

"Draw near to God; and he shall draw near unto you; cleanse your hearts. Verse 10 says "humble yourselves in the sight of God. He will lift you up; there is no shadow of shifting in Him; what He's said; He will do!"

"Thank you, Saints! Welcome to our throne room!" Hay ended and sat down in Dr. Sloans chair.

****

"I liked your sermon, Dad!" Harrison complimented.

"I did too, Dad!" Hay joined in.

"Well now, Aurelia and I liked it, too. Forty people came forth, My husband you were very commanding!"

"Well, I thank you all. Everytime I step up I feel more grounded; like it was meant to be."

The Chinaberry Tree

"I know you, Hay. You were great, a real good man even before you started preaching."

"The support of my 'lil family' means a lot to me," Hay said taking my hand.

****

Later Hay holed up in his study. We watched Disney; did not disturb him. So I wait. Somehow I knew he was further forging plans for our trek south; months have passed. He's a Midwest mogul; a full-time coach and athletic director; now a preacher of the Word. The other event that claims his attention is a return to see the farm, livestock, growing and gathering cash crops, hunting and fishing; just visiting with Uncle Joe Love's descendents. He is not distracted; just preoccupied.

****

Thirty-five years have blown by in our very busy lives. We have "a sure foundation"; three wonderful offspring and deep abiding faiths. In this grand scheme of things, I still press pen to paper; I am mindful of all I share. Thoughts, words, ideals shape lives. It is not hidden, but in one's face to be read, digested, analyzed, used and put into practice. If it is good, edifying and true; I have done my job. Writing is a talent from God Most High I've used ten times over. The residuals added to the support of my gift. I accepted it, and utilize it continually.

Doors. So many doors are opened top me; and I have not "burned" one bridge. Our Lord dwells in me; I pray for many that they be sustained in life; covered under the watchful eyes of guardian angels. It is a given for my babies' sake. I am a praying mother.

****

The Chinaberry Tree

Though I mentally admonish myself to cease. The eleven novels I've done are a mere drop in the bucket. Oh, cliché, where is thy end?! Other authors have produced many more than eleven. My bundle of joy Auri comes near; claims my attention. There are more interruptions with three children to tend; a husband to look after; a home to keep in tip top shape.

Aurelia tugs at my hand. "Mommie, pick it up!" I play the game.

"Who is it?"

"Pick it up, Mom!" So I obey, cradle and rock her in my arms; smell her distinctive baby smells. There are times I hold them all on my lap, savoring the life God has gifted us. I may be small in stature. Like Grandma Matilda, who also was diminutive; she'd position Carla, Shirl and me on her lap. So I do the same. They giggle and grin. I am happy at their nearness.

Young Hay offers, "Mom, we should be holding you! He is quite the young man at almost eight. They soon take leave of me, off to play games, do kid's play; and I am once again concentrating on the task at hand.

Time can stop; matters morph and change; yet God does not take your gifts. They are there for the using. My "latter days are far greater than my past"! Authoring is an indelible part of my life. Once I was one, solely on my own. Haywood came and brought family; my extended branch of our family. Now there are five of us plus Carla. As I reside closer to God I have not lost anyone else. My circle of friends have broadened and expanded. We watch out for all. People came into our lives positively for a reason. With Haywood I procreated. We've been fruitful and multiplied. I am never alone. It is my fervent plea that God has set our course.

The Chinaberry Tree

"Dwell in me, O God of Abraham

Lead and guide us in every way each day

Reveal stable visions, make them plain

Easy to discern; easier to relate

My faith, hope, charity of heart

Is strong in thee, O Ransom Jesus.

Please bless one and all

From eave to eave; door to door

House to house in peace and love

Healing; Lord, let healing

And restoration abound

Please forgive us every foible

Sins begone! May all pleas

Be heard and answered

This is my fervent prayer

Son Supreme, please cover us!"

"In my life be glorified! In my heart instill your Word." Summarily my way of life has encompassed many. Our unsullied life touches many more. I am now packaging my last novel to Densbury. Since I have come "a mighty long way"; it is tiltled the same: "A Mighty Long Way".

The Chinaberry Tree

Dare I say questions arise whether such peace and tranquility can continu "Apple carts" are upset; "monkey wrenches" get tossed in a pile; "stumblir blocks" bar pathways; and "Murphy's Law" continually plague our existences. various ways Murphy has penned: "If anything can go wrong; it will".

Another of Murphy's Laws is: "No good deed goes unpunished"; "If yc want something bad enough chances are you won't get it"; "Just when you thir things cannot get worse; they will"; and moreover: "Whoever has the gold, make the rules."

My rule is: "Some things are too good to last forever." Still I pray that thes negatives never come to pass. I looked up and Hay was beaming, coming at n with a ring of shiny keys.

"We're leaving in three days! Is that enough time to pack?"

"I've already begun, Hay. I'm ready if you are ready."

"My Lady, we have a new shiny custom van!"

"Okay! Let's do it!" I answered; my enthusiasm increased. In this I war what he wants.

THE SECRET OF THE TREE

PART IV

JUNE 2008

The Chinaberry Tree

Hay's penultimate plan has come to fruition. All systems are go! We are ready. The when, is now. When he'd tried to plant the Chinaberries in the Midwest; he'd been trying to supplant the great times. Just like a man, the noxiousness of the berries was of little concern. Finally he'd given in; we opted for two cherry trees instead. They are beautiful, pleasant and give off bunches of sweet deep red cherries. Our boys have deep red ruby mouths from ingesting so many of them. Their chores extended beyond gathering. They soon had to remove the pits they'd spit about the patio. I'd ferment the fruit, strain and drain, then add lots of sugar to my version of Cherry Wine.

My job is to tidy Hay's study. It's his way of inviting me inside. I wipe and shine trophies, heirlooms and desk ornaments, then stack papers. I pick up a letter on a second stack. It seemed like a summon for us to visit soon. I place the letter on top of the stack. The letter prompted me to begin packing for the children and myself.

Ferndale fisher, Aunt Carrie's son was mentioned quite often in passing. Dale is tall and statuesque, with long flowing salt and pepper hair. "Trees", I concluded; all of them trees. Opposites attract.

"We'll see you soon," I'd mouthed as I closed the study door.

****

Walking my land reminds me of our morning walks with Uncle Joe about the farm. Dale, Unc, and me out in the cool morn, connecting with the land. Condensation covers the field and many plants. Cool air has met the rays of just approaching sunrise. How many times have I made this walk; in touch with nature. Before entering home I stopped at the gate to get the mail. The fifth letter was from Johnston Station, Mississippi. Dale's uneven scrawl summoned us. At the patio I shed my shoes. The noise from the kitchen welcomed me. It's an almost everyday happening. I gave Jus' her mail, then stopped off at my study to put mine on the desk. All freshened up, I rejoined them.

"Flapjacks. I love flapjacks. Give me a pile, and some of that bacon and; some sausages. Come on, bow your heads!" I think my prayer included: 'Good Morning, Lord, thank you for another day, and this beautiful breakfast. Please bless those that have not. If they have not; send them by here, Lord. Through Jesus, Amen."

Boisterous. Jovial. Light-hearted, and much chewing. How I love Justine's flapjacks!

"That was grand, Lil' Woman!"

"I aim to please!" She answers engaging our sons in cleaning; and clearing the table. I embrace her.

The boys gave each other knowing looks. Aurelia clapped her hands squealing, "Daddee! Daddee!" She is truly her Daddy's girl.

****

"So much to do," I concluded, but took up Dale's letter first. There I let it stay for several days. Ferndale was extending a "come down and see us soon" invite. Later when Justine took the tour of our van she'd simply said: "Now we're going."

****

The road ahead seemed long and winding; over a thousand miles. We sang, played games, and talked, even listened to spirited tapes over and over again. So much I'd internalized every lyric. When we reached the mid-south at Memphis we were almost there, not far to go, about four hundred miles. The scenic route had changed considerably. I used to think of it as paradise. Strong tornadoes had ravaged the land in northern Mississippi. The green was less lush. I dialed Dale on the car phone, hands-free: 601-276-7682, runs tickertape through my mind. Some numbers you never forget. Much time has passed; and I still recall.

Three hours later we were negotiating the steep incline and grassy knoll sloping into the lush farm. Dale had tended it well. There he sat, tall in the saddle of a finely groomed golden Palomino. Commanding. Dresser of all we could see, he'd assumed the position Uncle Joe had been skeptical he could. Rows of crops were neatly turned and planted in the background to the left. He'd rotated them. To the right groves of peach, pear, and plum trees budded beautifully. The air was crisp and clear.

A minor replica of Dale, his son stood next to him. In his letters he'd made no mention of his son's mother, only that he was rearing Abraham Joseph to be a "man's man" on the farm. Now, Uncle Joe's handsome men of purpose. I looked and the Chinaberry still stood tall and sturdy; belying its years. Age had not hastened its decline. They came towards us, not even in a hurry. Weary; somewhat weary, we sat for a while watching their approach.

My mother made this trip every summer. Our Dad was less zealous about the trip. He is a real "city slicker", more comfortable in the Midwest. Mom taught us to love the South. Aunt Carrie Mae and Aunt Eliza embraced us in wonderful southern smells; especially "just baked" kitchen aromas; enveloping us in strong hugs.

The Chinaberry Tree

"Ya'll mighty big for ya'll's britches!" Aunt Carrie exclaimed. Just noting our increased sizes. Two weeks on the farm we'd grown even more. All that vitamin D and country cooking prompted that; we were tall and very developed; young men of strength, sporting great thick manes we'd allowed to grow long like Uncle Joe's.

My peace of belonging began here. It is the right place, stirring right feelings in me. The speckled black and white guinea fowl run free. They lurched about like "drunks" after ingesting the orangey brown berry bunches that fall from the Chinaberry Tree.

Yellow and white wrought chairs have fresh coats of paint. Horses graze nearby in the corral. The whole area is cut back to the expanse and thicket of the woods. "To keep the wild things at bay," Unc would always say. Everyone worked, including us for two weeks. When we'd start back, Unc would give Mel and I crisp hundred dollar bills.

"A good day's pay; for a good day's work, I always say!"

"Thanks, Uncle Joe!" We chorused.

It was the best of times during a simple existence. I'd saved the hundred until the eagle grinned. Forever. For seven years Mom herded us south. Then I became interested in sports. B-ball became my life; starred in by images of Cheerleader Justine Jones. Mother still made the trip a few years, apprehensive to leave Melvin and I. We kept the "home-fires burning" nicely. It was second nature to do the expected; take care of us; and our home.

He'd joke with me about Jus': "When you gonna make that move, Hay?"

The Chinaberry Tree

"Soon, brother, soon!" I'd answer; but every time I got near her I forgot I was a straight student.

****

"Note to Hay! Come back from Jamaica! Dale's at your window."

Automatically I pushed the down button; then opened the door instead, and stepped out. My cousin and I embraced with strong back pats.

"Well hello to you too, Haywood!"

"Been a long time, cous!"

"Time flies; and you made it!"

Jus' and the children piled out picking up Auri. Dale and I took suitcases, lugging them to the porch. Aunt Carrie squealed through the sieves of the screen, then bounded outside on the porch.

"Whoo-ee! Ya'll just too big for your britches!" I towered over her; but held her in a strong embrace.

"Okay. Just what you cookin', pretty lady?"

"All yo' favorites. Fresh chicken 'n' dumplings, green beans, and rice; peach-berry cobbler, and the sweetest ice tea ya'll ever tasted!"

"Now you know I love your sweet 'n-to-the-taste tea! How 'bout some of your great lemonade I've been craving all the way here?"

"I've got that, too!"

The Chinaberry Tree

"Can't wait, Auntie!" I enthused drawing Justine and the children along with us.

"Justine, Young Haywood, Harrison, and Aurelia meet Aunt Carrie Mae, and Cousin Fern-Dale Fisher."

"Now let's not leave out my son Abraham Joseph."

We all embraced then started up the steps. Great aromas wafted to my nostrils. For the next two hours we ate, caught up, and made plans. I look around me and I am stirred. My family has connected with my southern beginning. It's grand. I stand to excuse myself.

"I know where he's going," Jus' says.

"And where is that Lil' Woman'?"

"Why I know you, Hay. The Chinaberry Tree, right?"

"You are right!" Dale also rises and carries suitcases near the four bedrooms. He's added an addition. The farm house is neat tidy and sprawling. Each room large and accommodating. Jus' and the boys help clear the table. I bound down the steps two at a time en-route to the tree.

****

The creaky aged swing groaned from the weight of me. I moved to one of the larger wrought iron chairs. Peaceful. Evening was approaching, the sun dipping low. Dusk welcomed by a cacophony of insect noises.

"Unc, I'm here. Are you here?" I uttered softly. It seemed silly to be speaking into nothingness. The farm is he; though tended and dressed by Dale; he is it. Once more my mind began to drift. No one to interrupt me here.

The Chinaberry Tree

"You hear me, boy! The Lawd calls you, be ready to answer. Many are summoned; but few answer. The Lawd called me when I twenty, but I ran. Those fine yaller' gals called to me. That's trouble with a capital 'T'. Preachin' ain't conducive to playin' around. Some ignored that fact. Brought a whole heap o' trouble on themselves and others."

"Yield not to temptation; for yielding is sin; but each victory will help you to win! You wanna win don't you boy? Yeah, I can see it in you; you're a winner, Godwin!" I winced at his ignoring my given name.

"That's it! Conquer temptations; and the sky's the limit!"

"Unc, women are pretty, soft and nice to be around. How do you give up women?"

"Heh! Heh! You ask good questions boy! Anyways, go to church, study the scriptures, pay some dues; listen to good preachin'; just get closer to God. It all works out in the long-run."

"Is that all?"

"No. Be a good steward o'er every field, every animal the eye can see; cherish the land. All is a gift; on loan. For we bring nothing in this world; and we take nothing out of it. Though I love me some Gawd, not much draw me to that pulpit. I see a kinda move on some pastors. Some pine for their positions. Seems to be a seat of covetous scorn; they want what they do not have. Be careful of what you desire. You listenin', Godwin?"

"Yes, suh!"

The Chinaberry Tree

"But you, the Lawd gon' make many ways fo' you! No fence sittin' fo' you! It's all over you, Haywood! I hope I live to see it! Your life will be full of grace and prosperity. You shall holpen many! Bless you, My son!"

The screen door slammed jolting Uncle and startling Mel. Aunt Carrie's hands on her hips reminded me of a "ruffled clucking hen".

"Papa! Papa! Let these young men come in to supper. You're near starvin' them with all this talk! You, too! Come on! Rise and shine! Food's getting' cold!"

Laboriously he'd risen taking one step at a time. Mel and I caught each arm. After a few steps he'd waved us away to amble on his own. Unc did not live to see all he's predicted. His time to go; his departure came almost one year later. He'd been eulogized with great accolades. They referred to him as Reverend Joseph Love, touting his great love of God. He would have chuckled at that, but still received that edict. There's none perfect; he'd thought himself too imperfect.

Ferndale stuck close to the Love Farm; became its new tender of the sail. To all it seemed the way it should be.

****

Good smells and wonderful aromas of chicken stew in buttery dumplings, peach cobbler, snapped green beans, cornbread made me feel more famished than I'd recognized. We'd always respectfully sat and listened; forgetting the time. The more matters change; the more they remain the same. Just like old times I joined my family for supper.

My future has now connected with my southern past; the southeast have now met those formally from the Midwest. None needed prompting to join hands and "thank God" for the bounty set before us. "Elatron, be my gatekeeper! I am the winner, the preacher, father, helper of many; and the receiver of all he'd continually transferred to me."

I am his "heir apparent"; but Dale keeps the farm. Wealthy in my own right, I conclude it is the natural order of things. "God bless the man that cleaves close to Him; who obtains his own.

"Dale, you going to eat all those dumplings?" I ask bringing myself to the present activity.

"No, just most of them. You know how I love dumplings?" The joviality permeates the meal. My wife and three children seem at ease, I conclude as I gaze upon their shiny bright faces. Contented even.

"God is good!" I aver as I down my second glass of Aunt Carrie's precious lemonade.

It is a treasure she's always offered even when we were younger. Dale talking of graduation, listening to him on the phone with a myriad of young girls. Finally he'd settled. Began to go to etta Bena to take up agriculture. It was the natural order of matters.

****

"You're pretty good Haywood!" Dale complemented as we shot some hoops at the net.

"I'm a 'basketball man', cuz'!"

"Let's see what you got!" He'd challenged as we'd played three-on-three with Melvin.

The Chinaberry Tree

It was the best of times. Evening sounds surrounded us; dusk drew us inside, as lightening bugs began to flicker incandescently. We sat for a while on the porch.

****

"Just like 'old times' I'd concluded as the past and now become the second day of our trip. Our children settled near Justine's lap; she looked like a doze comin' on. The incessant ring of the phone interrupted the serenity. Dale rose to answer and stayed inside. After a time we all rose to ready for bed. There I cradled her in my arms.

"Ya' know, Hay you draw great people into your life."

"You don't say?!"

"I sure do! I love your family; Solomon and Georgia; Mel and Beverley; and Mark and Sherita; et al their little families. I really adore you, 'Godwin'; she'd joked. I had other ideas than a new strain of conversation.

"Don't start nothin'; won't be nothin', Hay. We are not waking up this house!"

"Oh, I don't know. I thought we'd play a game of quiet!"

"Quit, Hay! Go to sleep!"

"Yes, ma'am!"

****

The relentless sunshine, and all that activity lulled me to sleep for hours; in the protective cocoon of loving arms. Dale has carried on, developed, and now oversees all Uncle Joe had in mind. He'd groomed us all quite well. Boys have now become "men of purpose", iron has sharpened iron; 'man sharpened men' in all their bearings. The end has justified the means. In all his teachings; he has shaped us. We are, Dale, Mel, and I are 'mighty men' capable of managing much.

"Way to go, Unc'!" I think as we began our third day on the Love Farm.

The Chinaberry Tree

FERNDALE'S

FOIBLES

PART V

The Chinaberry Tree

Young Harrison and Hay blasted the HDTV. They giggled and grinned at reruns of age old cartoons from the seventies.

"He's so silly!" Harrison laughed.

"Prunetta!" Another character exclaimed. We stood for a time watching them watch Bugs and Elmer cut up.

"Now those were real cartoons!" Haywood said joining them on the floor. Aunt Carrie came in yawning.

"Now what's all this racket? Breakfast ready soon," she'd said entering the dining room; and was soon plopping two large skillets on Bunson burner eyes. I joined her cracking a dozen eggs, tossing in some cheese and chopped ham. In moments omlets were turning, bubbling nicely in one of the skillets.

Chatter. There was always amiable chatter and the feel of goodwill. I looked out at the corral as I poured orange juice. Someone else had risen early. The rider alit from the golden horse. He removed his cropped hat, struck the side of his pants. Long wavy salt 'n' pepper hair spilled over his shoulder. My Hay walks about our land; Dale rides. He wiped his brow with a blue and white bandana, then his face.

"Justine," Aunt Carrie called softly.

"The batter's ready," I said absently; passing her the bowl. Soon the backdoor slammed and Dale entered the half bath room.

Carrie chuckled. "Nothing stops Dale from his morning ride. He's more like papa than he'll ever know," Carrie informed. Papa used to say: "…and He gave us

The Chinaberry Tree

dominion over all the animals; and every living thing...Said God didn't mind if he'd check up on all on loan to him."

"Your father must have been really astute!"

"Now what that mean, Justine? Talk simple to me, girl"

"Very smart; a good teacher; all of the above!" I'd answered.

"He was that!" She'd ended and made three stacks of pancakes of huge circumference.

We met at the huge table. Dale joined us with horsey smells, liniment, and outdoorsy smells. Hay and Dale sat opposite each other at the head. We bowed as Dale offered prayer:

> "Good mornin', Lord! Fine mornin', Lord! Thanks for rest, the great meal that shall help us stand every test of the day. Bless these cooks, and all the partakers; bless those that have not. Ever thankful, Lord Jesus!
>
> Amen"

We all chorused "Amen", then passed, took portions, and dug into another great breakfast. My husband talked among his people. He is as at home here, as he is on our estate. He is an extraordinary man co-existing with others in ordinary circumstances. Within the personage of those two men, I have met Joseph Love. He is so much a part of both of them. "Our God sits high outside time. He sees our beginnings, the middle passage; and He knows our ends. I conclude and delve into the mound of food on my plate; feeding Aurelia who's seated next to me. This is a "Kodak" moment. I shall carry these images with me forever.

The Chinaberry Tree

Once I was one, alone with only Carla; now I have Haywood, our circle of friends; his brother Melvin and Beverley, their twins; and many friends; have extended to Young Hay, Harrison, and Aurie; and finally I am connected to Hay's southern connection: Aunt Carrie, Cousin Dale, Abraham, and Willy Bell. My "one" has now become many. This is so powerful! I know that God has orchestrated every nuance of my life. My "latter has become greater than my past. We are in favor with God. How wonderful it is to be connected to many who love and revere the Creator!"

The extolling conversation takes us to ten o'clock. Soon some excuse themselves. Our boys help clear and soon return to the TV. We all heard the car negotiate the incline. It must have been a "stick"; I could hear gears scratching. It soon stopped on a level place next to the van. A beautiful girl climbed out drawing two suitcases after her. When she bent to pick them up, her long thick hair almost touched her waist. Dale went to the porch stepped off and effortlessly lifted the cases, then took them to the fourth bedroom. Carrie hugged her. "Justine, this is Dale's girl, Willy Bell; home from college. She's going to be a lawyer."

"Nice to meet you Willy," I said.

"I'm hungry, Gran! You got breakfast left?"

"Oh, I think we can find a few morsels for you!"

"Dad? Dad!" She called

Once more we joined Willy at the table. Carrie was shelling butter beans and passed me a large bowl. As one meal ended; preparation for another soon began. The midday meal was interrupted by the glee of children. Hay was taking them all to Magic Mountain.

The Chinaberry Tree

"Skeeballs!" Young Hay squealed. That game seemed to be a favorite.

"Mom, you and Auri going?" Harrison asked hopefully.

"She's not quite ready for skeeball. We'll watch a little TV and snooze in the rocker."

"Well, okay, but we'll be back real soon. You won't even miss us," he reasoned.

"You can bring me some popcorn; and some cotton candy, okay?"

"It's a deal, Mom!"

"Let's go!" Hay called. They were soon loaded into the van. I took Auri in the kitchen for apple juice and honey-bear grahams. The changing images, and the drone of voices brought on naps. My last thought was ,"I've wanted to see this!"

****

Something scratched me on my forehead and I slapped at it. It felt foreign and unnatural. So I slapped at it again opening my eyes. "Ooh! What?!" The heavy odor of horse and sweat met my sense of smell.

"I'm sorry, Justine I didn't mean to startle you or the babe. You looked so peaceful. Like something out of Country Living Magazine..." His voice trailed off; and I sat up straight, cradling Auri and putting the chair back into upright position.

"I thought you went with the others."

"No. I had much to tend to over in the north field. No time fore all those kiddy games."

The Chinaberry Tree

I rose slowly bringing Auri along with me. She was cranky and began to whimper, her afternoon nap interrupted.

I'll just take her for a walk," I said feeling real uneasy about the scratchy kiss on the forehead.

"Looks like that contraption was watchin' you 'stead of you watchin' it!" He hung his jacket and hat near the door then went into the bathroom.

The opportunity arose for me to distance myself further. We went outside I carried her to a level place then set her down. We walked further up the incline. Every now and again Auri stopped to pick up small objects and toss them askew without any follow through.

"No! No, baby!" I said. "Come with Mommie. "Finally we reached the entrance. I hoped it was Hay. The occupants waved and passed on by. We ogled other passers-by for a while, then slowly started down the paved incline. Dale sat on the porch still staring. I didn't want to sit on the porch with dale, so I slowed our pace. I did not feel "chummy".

Hay's van turned into the entrance just as we'd reached the level place. Relief flooded me. We moved to the side and waved. Harrison bounded out shoving a box of popcorn not quite full in my hand; and melty cotton candy in the other.

"I hadda' eat some, Mom!"

"That's okay. You did good!"

I shared the treat s with Aurelia. Cotton candy smeared cherry red on her smacking lips. She kept licking her lips. Abraham teased her with a southern ditty:

The Chinaberry Tree

"Lizard! Lizard! Show me yo'

Pocket book and I won't steal you..." Auri squealed as he picked her up. With the chameleon it's a sensory thing; with Auri it was the sweet taste. Haywood took her and swooped me up as if we'd weighed light as eider down.

"How're my girls? Did you miss me?" He said eyeing Dale on the porch. He hadn't moved.

"We did. We watched TV, then took a nap. The house was quiet til Dale came home."

"How 'bout we go see Casino Royale? I hear it's pretty good!"

"It's a date! What time?"

"Oh, sevenish," he said evenly still watchin' Dale.

"Can't wait!" I said then caught up with Carrie. "Wanna watch my gang while Hay and I go to the movies?"

"That'll be easy. They'll sleep like lambs after baths and a story."

"I see you know exactly what to do."

"Who else raised Dale, Willy and Abraham?"

"You're going to say 'you'!"

"For sho'!"

****

I'm a James Bond fiend; even if it is a remake!"

The Chinaberry Tree

"He doesn't disappoint, all fierce and ferocious!"

"Tell me, Jus'! What happened?!"

"Dale kissed me on the forehead. Awakened us with a start. Auri got cranky, so I took her for a walk."

"You want me to talk to him?" We were almost back to the farm.

"No. I can avoid him for another day and a half."

"Well. I will tell him to keep his mitts off my woman."

"I'm okay."

****

When you know whose you are; being with someone else never crosses your mind. It did not cross mine. I belong to God; and Hay Jennings, Jr. We met everyone in the living room sans the children that had been bathed, storied, and bedded down.

Hay is so transparent. "Is my honey tired?" He'd asked, took my hand and drew us to our room.

"Let's bathe together, save some water," he'd suggested. The invitation was not about saving water.

"Let's take this shower together…"

"You are not enticing me."

"It's not a sin. We are one, Jus'!"

"I know that!" I grabbed a towel and left his amorous self there in the stall.

The Chinaberry Tree

He followed me singing: "Who can you, who can, you run to?"

"You are so silly! Quit it, Haywood!"

I pulled up the covers. Auri stood in the door. "Mom! Daddee! Can I sleep with you?" We were laughing heartily. She padded across the room and scrambled next to me.

"I heard noises!"

I'm sure she'd heard us, the whippoorwills, cadidids, tree frogs and such; but mostly us.

"Daddy?"

"Uh huh?"

"How do you get used to all these animals?"

"Well, most are pretty tame."

"I don't know. They nip and bite."

"How 'bout we pet a few tomorrow?"

"They won't hurt me?"

"There's nothin' to fear. I'll be there."

"You goin' fishin' with Cousin dale?"

"Fishing is fun. We'll take bamboo poles and a pail of wiggly, squiggly worms to the pond, bait our hooks and catch dinner. Mommie, will you go also?"

The Chinaberry Tree

"Okay. This place is loaded with Southeast China imports. Let's see Kudzu, Chinaberries, bamboo and moss."

"Jus' I 'think' that came from Spain. You know Spanish Moss."

Aurelia joined in. "Our cherry, apple, and orange trees are nice."

"You are so observant, girl!" She yawned and jumped out of bed.

"I thought you were with us for the night."

"I'm okay. Not scared anymore. Tuck me in, Dadee!"

Our sheets smelled sun-kissed, now warmed by our 98.6's. We talked far into the night.

"Auri okay?"

"She's just missing her room; her bed."

"Are we lonesome for ours as well?"

"Pretty much; but anywhere is home with you!" He'd answered holding me close. The thrill is not gone!

Incredibly inevitably it is so!

****

Hay and Abraham cleaned the brim, sunfish and crappies we'd caught at the pond. After an hour they brought them inside and put them in the sink.

We had a real "London" meal of fish 'n' chips, and slaw. Time passed fast. We were almost packed ready to go, the next day. Our seven day stay was almost done. I am glad we have done this.

THE TREE GIVES UP IT'S SECRET

PART VI

The Chinaberry Tree

If I told her she wouldn't believe me. In deep sleep Justine snores. She is soft, beautiful, golden. I watch her sleep. Unc often told us to "leave those 'yaller' gals alone". Too late, Unc! She is my world and she is golden. I moved my arm that feels numb. She stirs, but does not awaken.

Quickly I dress, and exit the room. I go to meet the Lord on the morn. On these walks I petition the Lord Most for all on loan to me. This morn I had to see if Unc's secret place in the huge aged tree has survived weather and wear.

The house was silent save the minor creak of house floorboards. I glanced at the clock. Six thirty. Hen's were clucking, and roosters crowing as I stepped up my pace en-route to the tree.

The Chinaberry Tree stood tall and silent with no remarkable change to it. The dawn's light gave an overbearing aura. I moved around the tree three times stopping with my back to the fence. I allowed my hand to spiral downward to a rough enclosed space. I rapped on the smooth center surface forcefully. The panel slid back. I pushed further; then rummaged inside. My hand connected with frayed papers and four plastic packs. A cloud of dust surfaced. I coughed dryly. Particles can reach any space. Some dust had collected inside though the center panel seemed airtight.

"Look close, Godwin! Im'po'tent stuff here! I'mo share this whole place with you! It is blessed by Gawd! Men who fear and love the Lord must tend it. Long as it's tended, seeded, preserved it's blessed. Live yo' life in Gawd. The Lorg spell it out in Deuteronomy: 'teach yo' whole household. One day you run this farm I'm speakin' on you, boy! Live yo' life and learn well. A man who trusts in Gawd goes far, accomplishes much. This farm be yours, Haywood." All he'd said was true. There is much on loan to me. He'd used my given name at last; not Godwin, but Haywood.

****

Sometimes one does not always get what's set forth for them; but can through other means receive a "facsimile" of that intended gift. I stood there with papers in my hands that would shake up many lives. Unc thought Dale would never shape up; but he has. He expanded it and tends it well.

Sometimes one in the right place may obtain by proxy what has been set aside for others. Biblically Esau's birthright was stolen by his desire for a "bowl of beans" and trickery by mother and brother. Dale stuck and stayed, and I rarely came after seven years. In B-ball heaven I'd gained much, taking a different route. I still had hope, tenacity and all it took to survive. I looked through the packets in my hands. Money.

The laborious scrawl of Unc's writing looked like faded chicken scratches "peanut brown" scrawled on worn paper; the black ink faded. The money in plastic did not discolor.

"*Godwin (Haywood) this Love Farm I leave to you. Your Mama Myrtle married a good man, tall and deliberate as we, I knew her mind. They settled in Sullivan. I did visit a few times, but could not tarry long. I had to get back to this land. Ever since you were four she brought you back to this land. So I counsel you under the tree; marked you in my remembrance. You polite, always sit and listen, even query me. All was a good sign. I knew you'd be a great man. You are a great man, ain't you, Haywood?* "Yaller gals" *troubled my soul, but I simmer down and marry, raise yo' mama Myrtle, Carrie Mae, Toby, and Jeff; even take on Ferndale, Carrie's love child.*

The Chinaberry Tree

Family is all that counts in the scheme of things. Keep yo' family together movin' in the right way. Grow up "great trees". I leave this place to you. Carrie and Dale may stay as long as they like. No matter. This place I leave to you, Haywood Jennings, Jr. of Sullivan, Michigan.

Being of sound mind at eighty three, I grant it to you, and fifteen thousand. Three policies shall benefit my children Carrie, Eliza, Ferndale, and Myrtle. People's Life & Casualty is the handler of the ample policy.

Money is fleeting like sifting sand; here today; gone tomorrow, but this farm and its wealth remains forever when it's filled with love.

Gawd bless you, Son

Much Love

Preacher Joseph H. Love

May 26, 1993

****

The will fluttered to the ground and blew against the tree. I sank next to it, picked it up and folded it. Tears flowed in rivulets scalding my face. Cool morn air met warm tears and seeped into my mouth. I quickly wiped my face on my sleeve, and put the letters in my jacket pocket. I tugged at the circular center; tugged it back in place. How could I upset or uproot Carrie Mae and Dale's lives? I have so much. More than any knows. I slipped the plastic packets in my pockets, then came around the tree; moving towards the farm. Jus' stood at the steps calling to me. Her voice sounded foreign; caught up in vastness. I stepped towards it, eager to be near her.

The Chinaberry Tree

"Hay, where are you?"

"Right here, hon," I answered as I came around the side of the house; met her at the steps then embraced her. "I'm right here. I've never left you!"

"You walk away all the time. Like you can't do the same thinking in my presence."

"The brisk walks help my appetite." She kissed my cheek standing on the top step.

"You been crying?"

"That's just dew...morning dew." I hedged.

"Well come to breakfast. We've been waiting."

"Will do! Let me freshen up a bit!" I said making a beeline for our room. Quickly I put papers and packaged money into the zippered side of my luggage, and locked it. I soon donned a clean fresh shirt, took off my boots and joined them at the table; goodwill and great food on my mind.

It is the right order of things. I have a part of Uncle Joe's legacy; I will visit from time to time, but Carrie and Dale are the farm's caretakers. Love has perpetuated this bond. It's one I refuse to break. I have been granted much. I can afford to be magnanimous. Joe Love's legacy is sound.

The chair I chose at the other end of the table scraped loudly as I sat down.

"Cuz' Dale, keep yo' mitts off my woman!" Startled, Dale stuttered.

"Cuz'! Jus', ya'll know I didn't mean a thang! We all family!"

The Chinaberry Tree

"You better know it!" I said digging into Carrie's sumptuous breakfast vittles.

The next day we loaded up the van and headed for the Midwest. "By Sunday we'll be home," I told Dale on Saturday noon. They all waved us up the incline and onto Summit Road.

****

Three weeks have passed. We're home again. Justine opened one of ten books Densbery sent. A picture of the bluff and valley, and a single figure standing on the precipice of the hill. I took one and thumbed through it. "A Mighty Long Way" is a three hundred paged novel.

"It's sort of like an autobiography," she'd shared.

"Am I in it?"

"You're all over it!"

"Jus' when did you take this picture?"

"Once when I followed you. All was in bloom. I wanted to see if you were meeting Betty Deer out here!"

We both laughed. "You know that was high school."

"I know."

"Uncle Joe left me something. I want to share it with you. My Lil' Woman!" After retrieving the packets, we counted it together.

"It's fifteen thousand dollars!"

The Chinaberry Tree

"What about the beginning for a trust for our Lil' Trees?"

"I can think of nothing better," she'd agreed. The boys burst through the door.

"Mom! Harrison called me that forbidden word!"

"We're home!" we'd mouthed. Hay spoke firmly to Harrison.

"Let's not use that word, Harrison. Don't call your brother names!"

"He called me short!"

"Well, you think he meant..."

"He meant it, Dad!"

"Young Hay, what did you really want to say to your brother?" He gave Young Hay that steady stare.

"Harrison, you're growing taller everyday!" He said seeking his Father's approval, and wanting to be off the hook.

"So I think 'Submissions' have no end!" Then I ponder, "Shall I always be like this?"

Matters left alone to their own devices do not improve. I marvel that "My Hay" has his pulse on every aspect of our lives; even his franchises and the athletics of Beason County. He's even requested another playmate for Aurelia.

"Request noted, Brother Minister," I'd answered, though only lukewarm to the idea.

The Chinaberry Tree

Hay's mission is to win many to Christ; to snatch them from the gaping abyss of the nether world.

I'm frankly fully aware of what's promised to those who seek after this "great light of the world." The desires of our hearts are overflowing. Our children's children are duly covered; blessed immeasurably.

The Chinaberry Tree

EPILOGUE

Our social gatherings have evolved; our "circle of interests" expanded. Betty and Fred are a couple now; and among our closest friends. At times Hay doesn't slow down; is driven even! He draws many. Gone is the revelry, jazzy music, and such. We simply enjoy moments shared with many.

Our offspring are taught much. They have tremendous wealth to inherit. My husband is on a mission to prepare them. This mansion we share always seems to be filled with friends and family.

"Are we having service in our home? It sure seems so! I tell Hay our fourth child is on the way and he exclaims, "Ain't no shame in my game!"

In June of two thousand nine we return to consort with the Southern connection. When I observe him near that aging stately tree I get this feeling he's home again. There he sits for hours watching the "moveable feast" of animals; even people. From time to time he and Dale and Abraham play ball with our boys. Aurelia hangs out with me sensing another child is developing inside me.

As long as we stay close to God we shall dwell in peace; and that peace shall help us triumph over any calamities that arise. In the meantime; in between time we shall be likened to the Five Virgins of Matt 25:1-13. "The Kingdom of Heaven is likened to ten virgins who took their lamps and went out to meet the bridegroom. Five were wise, and five were foolish. The unready took lamps, but no oil, the wise took lamps, and vessels of oil.

All slumbered and slept as the bridegroom was delayed. Vs 6. aver: "and at midnight a cry was heard: 'Look the bridegroom comes; go out and meet him. All virgins rose up and trimmed their lamps. But the five foolish were unprepared and said to the wise: 'Give us some oil; for our lamps go out!"

"Is your light low? When he comes will you be ready? Don't let Him catch you with your light not shining!" Pray, praise and honor Him with Thanksgiving. Rise up early, anoint yourself with blessed oil. The anointing oil destroys yokes. Fill your lamp of life with goodness, love, peace, mercy, kindness, and tenacity. Trim your wicks that they may burn brightly from this oil you continually provide. Haven't you heard, we who love and obey Him are "the lights on a thousand hills; the very salt of the earth!"

Jesus is waiting; patiently waiting for our readiness. Live your life in His light. Let us run with endurance the race set before us. Hebrew 12:1-2 admonishes us to lay aside sin, endure as we run the race set before us." Finally, brethren, "Look to Jesus; the author and finisher of our faith.

Will the Lord say "Too Late", or will He invite you in? The final implication is verse thirteen of Matthew 2:5. "Therefore watch, for you neither know the day or the hour which the Son of Man is coming."

Summarily, we all join in a love song to our Lord; 'standing so close together that one cannot fall for the other'. So we 'come on up a little higher' cheered by this devout man of God! Hallelujah! Glory! Amen.